LOVE AND WAR:

THIS IS THEIR STORY...

D1521164

JARED THURMON

Book Design by HMDgfx.com

Contents

INTRODUCTION

Moments Matter

Do you know where you were on 9/11? What do you remember? How about when the Challenger blew up or when President Kennedy was shot?

We all have moments in life—deciding moments, pivotal moments, remarkable moments—maybe it was that first kiss; that one holiday; that one night; that special day; that first day.

I remember one Christmas morning, opening up a Nintendo and feeling life could never be better than this moment. I remember this one basketball game in high school where it seemed I couldn't miss a shot. I remember that sick feeling in my stomach sitting inside the Disney castle as I prepared to ask my girlfriend to become my wife. I remember the night we got married—I remember it very well [big smile]. I remember the moment my daughter was born.

Life is about moments. Sometimes those moments aren't always positive. Sometimes there are moments that can't be comprehended. I remember one of those moments: a call from someone telling me about an accident in which my dad had been involved, prompting me to come quickly. I knew, somehow, deep down, as I drove to the hospital, he didn't make it.

We don't question the highs in life, but we sure do question the lows. Why cancer? Why don't they love me anymore? Why did they have to die? There is something in us that doesn't understand the tragic moments, especially when we can't make much sense of them.

Many today believe for one reason or another that we are on the verge of another decisive moment, a collective moment for mankind. We have our theories, ideas, opinions, speculations, agendas, and conspiracies. Some see a climate catastrophe; others an erosion of the moral and social fabric of society; and still others—well, at least 3 to 4 billion of those who identify as Christians or Muslims—as some sort of last days.

Regardless of whether you see the world from the perspective of the right or left, religious or atheist, black or white, wrong or right, there is a growing sense that we are on the verge of something unprecedented.

They say those who don't learn from history are doomed to repeat it. Mark Twain once said, "History may not repeat itself, but it sure does rhyme."

What I'd like to talk to you about in the next few pages is something that I think will make your life better. Is all the information I'm going to share with you good news? No, not all. Is it all bad news? No, not at all.

I don't want you to have any misconceptions. The purpose of this book is to make sense of a story; to put all the random ideas you may have heard before into a coherent narrative.

I've found the way we feel about something is often closely tied to our perspective. Therefore, to be truly transparent, what I'm going to share with you is from my perspective: a white, straight, married, American male with a Judeo-Christian upbringing. Now, if I'm being totally transparent, it's at the feet of white, straight, married, American Judeo-Christian men that most of the sins and sorrow of the American experiment lay.

Before you think that there may be something more important to listen to or watch, give me a few more seconds to make my case as to why I think you should read this book.

Today, we live in a world where a growing majority of the leaders of our nations identify as Christian. There are more people among us who identify as followers of Jesus than any other group on earth. "Christianity" is the largest cult, club, corporation, conglomeration, cacophony—or whatever you want to call it—of people on the planet.

Therefore, it's not just that two out of every seven of us identify as Christian; the real point I want you to hear me make is that the growing majority of leaders on our planet identify as Christian. Is this good news? Or is it bad news?

One argument could be that it's good news—that Christians are supposed to be nice people like the one they worship, Jesus—so it should be a good thing, but do we see that consistency of kindness across the board? No. And we don't in any religion.

The other side of the coin says, "No, this is bad news"—bad news if we don't believe in God and therefore disagree with the values of these persons in power; bad news if we are of another faith and don't agree with the tenets of Christianity; bad news to even some Christians because if there is one thing that is very clear, it is this: Christianity has not been homogeneous since the day it was founded. There has constantly been persecution amid the community of faith we call "Christian." In fact, Christianity is more guilty of persecution and waging war under the banner of the cross than any other group on earth. This includes persecution against both those within and without.

However, the reason I think this conversation is important is because whether we like it or not, whether we are Christian or not, the mingling of religion and government (church and state) is a threat to all people. The evidence is clear that the world was ruled by an empire that was ruled by religion for nearly 1,260 years. History identifies this time as the Dark Ages. Just ask the Mohammedans, or as we call them today, the Muslims, if this community called "Christian" has always represented its founder, Jesus, with love and not war.

That mingling of church and state—religion and government—is happening at a level that is unprecedented today. What you're going to hear me tell you will shock you. Let me test it out.

I believe the Bible is a lesson book on how to live our lives in the happiest and most sustainable way, but that very same book also seems to clearly foretell the dangers of mixing religion and politics (church and state). In fact, we don't need to look very hard to see that Jesus Himself states that His church, the movement He started 2,000 years ago, would turn on Him and become His greatest enemy.

It was that paradigm shift that revolutionized the way I saw the world. It's that perspective that you owe to yourself to understand so that you aren't deceived by whatever is thrown at you in this era of people claiming whatever they don't agree with as "fake news."

Here's how I see it. Most of the world has been told only half the story, or less, regarding a character known as Jesus, with some cherry-picked ideas that form the basis of many sects and divisions of Christianity.

When's the last time you tuned in to a show or movie in the middle of it, saw just enough to be confused, and turned it off. Then if someone said, "Hey, did you see that movie," you replied, "Well, I tried to watch it, but I watched some of the middle of it, and honestly I had to turn it off; it was so bad and made no sense." I think that's the best way to describe society's reaction to religion and specifically the story of the man named Jesus.

Just imagine: could it be possible that sinister people hijacked the story of Jesus? People who claimed to be His followers, but in reality, are His greatest enemies? What if they cherry-picked some things they wanted to say, made up the rest, and did all of this to enslave the masses and keep them controlled?

C'mon, we've seen it in the best movies. The bad guy isn't someone we hate all the time; he's actually likable sometimes and has redeeming qualities; but in the end, we realize he is so evil.

However, that's the key: we see the end. What if I could save you the time and headache of researching the history of Christianity, it's foundation of Judaism, the many sacred writings that both of these communities of faith hold dear, and show you the story from beginning to end so you could at least say, "Now, for the first time in my life, I understand the full story of these religions. I see why they are good, bad, or corrupt and why I like, dislike, or disdain that for which they stand."

Wouldn't you want to be able to understand why 2.5 billion people profess to believe something when perhaps they really don't understand how it started or, in this day and age, why so many leaders on earth are seemingly converging, working together, and positing their ideas, beliefs, and—what if you could learn from history where we may be headed? If, after all, history repeats and is a lesson book, how could we benefit from knowing the trend of tomorrow?

Once I put the pieces together of how the story is said to have begun, where it went off track, and where it's headed, I began to make sense of so many things in the world today. I began to understand why there is such a tension between Christian Americans and the rest of the world as it relates with climate change. I began to understand why America puts so much of its money into the military industrial complex. I began to make sense of why we are becoming a surveillance state.

I wouldn't be doing my honest part as a citizen of this planet if I didn't share with you what I have learned. If our roles were reversed, I would want you to do the same for me.

And here's the good news. I don't expect you to see everything the same way as I do at the end of this book. However, you will be informed more than ever before; you will have puzzle pieces that answer questions about which many are wondering but on which they can't quite put their finger.

You will be able to see one thing very, very clearly: why, in the midst of an age of progress and secularization, America is becoming more and more controlled in the courts and halls of government by persons identifying as Christian, yet not adhering to the principles and ideologies of their founder, Jesus.

If anything has piqued your interest, I invite you to join me as we make sense of all this before it's too late.

EPISODE 1

Coup d'éJah

This story starts up there; out there; in another place; on another planet.

There are different names for this place: Jannah, Paradise, Zion, Elysium, Utopia—but for the sake of our story, let's call it Jannah, if that's ok with you. What's written about this place makes it sound pretty amazing. If we could take trips there today, we would see a lot of hashtags and selfies from #Jannah.

Life there is not naked babies floating in the clouds. Life there is not a man with 70 virgins. In fact, what's described is life a lot like what we experience today, at least if we removed war, death, killing, affairs, disease, famine, and environmental destruction—all the things that fall under the heading of selfishness. It's kind of hard to imagine, but go with me there. What are the best moments we can imagine here and now imagine a place without all the bad?

The story goes like this: Everything was amazing! There are many planets with intelligent life, beings that don't get sick or ever taste death; the best food, the best parties, the most amazing music, experiences, friendships ... you name it, they had it all.

This galactic community, if you will, had one principle—one law to which all intelligent beings were subject. This, we are told, is the way it always had been. As long as everyone abided by this principle, all was well.

That principle was very clear: None lives for oneself. In other words, no one is to live selfishly. Some have described it more succinctly: love! As long as this one idea, this one principle, was lived, all was well.

However, that's really where our story begins.

As friends were visiting friends, eating with friends, traveling with friends, listening to music with friends, at the beach with friends, diving with friends, flying with friends—news broke out that a coup was under way in the capital city of Jannah. There had been whispers of something like this in the air, but few thought it could ever really happen.

The ambassador—the prime minister—the one to whom all looked up for his wisdom, beauty, and talent—Lucifer—was now leading this revolt.

The Administration of Jannah apparently had a meeting, a private meeting to which Lucifer was not invited. He thought he deserved a place at the table. How could him not being invited to a meeting result in a coup?

Well, later on, we learn that the meeting to which he wasn't invited was a meeting to discuss what plan should be carried out if any of the high intelligences of Jannah were to violate the law of love and walk in the path of selfishness. It hadn't happened before, but the meeting was held in case it ever did.

You can understand why Lucifer wasn't invited to that meeting. Well, we can understand now, but not in the moment. In the moment, the idea of revolt discussed in this private meeting was a secret, a mystery whose possibility had been hidden for ages.

I'll explain. The day of the meeting, Lucifer left and began to have a lot of side conversations throughout the coming days and months. He knew better but slowly began to choose to go his own way. He didn't feel he was treated fairly. Today, we would call it a coup, but we might have called it anarchy or, as they called it, a revolution.

It didn't happen overnight. There were those conversations; you know the kind: "Hey, did you hear ..."; "Hey, what do you think about ..."; subtle, slow, deliberate; where rumors grow, wounds fester, and discontent spreads like a virus. Imagine if you and I were there in the moment.

Lucifer begins to assert that within us all are godlike qualities, and we were being held down and needed freedom. Under the campaign of offering true freedom, many of the inhabitants of Jannah were perplexed.

Finally, after many conversations and campaign speeches, it finally came to a head. A meeting was called in the capital, where some things were clarified. Michael, one of the Administrators, was declared equal with another Administrator, whom we will call Jah. This was kind of understood, but for some reason, it needed to be made clearer. Lucifer bowed with all the rest, but soon afterward, stated he was willing to serve under Jah, but not Michael.

Around this time, the discussion arose that a new species of beings would be created. Much like how our best and brightest in Silicon Valley are on the verge of quantum computing, wetware, and artificial intelligence, where one day soon we may not be able to distinguish the difference between a human and a machine, these machines with human-like intelligence will be the dawn of a new era.

Well, in a similar but inarguably grander way, it was decided that a new species would inhabit the blue planet we now call earth. It was decided that mankind would be a new and distinct order. That's right, designers from another realm would have their hand in creating life. Lucifer wanted to take the lead and be involved with the design and rollout of the project, but it was decided that Michael would be the one to lead out.

Lucifer thought he was the favorite to take this lead role, and in many respects he was. The various ranks and divisions in Jannah took orders from him.

There were many in the city who weren't sure who was right. Could it be that perhaps they were being limited or repressed? Did they really have freedom like they had thought? You know that feeling you get when you have been so sure of something, then for some reason, you start to question all your assumptions?

Did they really enjoy freedom, or were they being manipulated? Was this real or a simulation? Lucifer called all the citizens together and told them that all the liberty they had enjoyed was at an end.

A new ruler had been appointed over them, whom they, from then on, must serve like slaves! Lucifer stated that he had called them all together to assure them that he would no longer submit to this invasion of his rights and theirs; that he would never again bow down to anyone; that he would take the honor, which should have been conferred upon him, upon himself and be the commander of all who would submit to follow him and obey his voice.

It sounded like it made sense, but there was clearly contention.

One contingent argued that nothing had changed. Lucifer was still in charge. Michael had existed before their kind ever did. They had no reason to believe anything would change. However, doubt began to creep up into many minds. Private conversations began to be had all over. For a time, it seemed like Lucifer was seeking to promote the peace and stability of the government. Many couldn't tell for the longest time where he stood. All of his points seemed to make sense, but after a while, you could just tell something was brewing.

One account describes a conversation Lucifer had with one of the citizens of Jannah. This citizen expressed that he had some issues with the Administration. He didn't want to sound undecided, so naturally he showed sympathy for Lucifer's cause and told him of his support.

However, after conversations like this and others, Lucifer would take these same words to other leaders in the city and used them to try and show how many were joining his cause while remaining publicly neutral.

At one point, the majority of the citizens of Jannah were on the side of Lucifer, but somehow, he played down his role in the brewing revolution. After quite a bit of time had passed, the moment came when Lucifer shared that he had had enough.

Millions marched to the capitol to declare that what they could not gain by persuasion and politics, they would gain by force. And here's the thing: there had been senate meetings; Michael had pleaded over many occasions that He was not out to remove anyone's liberty, and if things weren't restored to peace, war would break out; so they had been warned.

The citizens of Jannah didn't even know what war was. It had never happened before, so I dare say the gravity of the moment wasn't fully comprehended until it was too late.

At the capitol, Michael and Lucifer made clear what their sides of the issue were and that once and for all, everyone would need to make a decision as to whose side they were joining. On this occasion, it wasn't just the citizens of Jannah, but also all the leaders of all the interstellar systems, who were present as witnesses.

There were rumors that if his arguments were clear enough, Lucifer hoped to win the hearts of even the districts and become the leader of all realms. He argued that the citizens of Jannah needed no law.

Reports say that you could hear shouting and weeping as each side faced each other. At one point, the majority were on Lucifer's side, and he declared that with a simple vote, the majority would vote him as supreme leader. He mocked the idea of how Jah, Michael, and the "slaves of Jannah" would continue on without the presence of the majority and leave such a void in the capitol.

However, even in that moment, many one-on-one conversations were taking place, and many regained reason and conscience and stated they would rejoin the ranks of Jah and Michael.

At that moment, Jah stood up after all the citizens had been given plenty of time to make their choice, and it was shown that now the majority supported Michael. However, Jah stated that the peace of all realms was because of the covenant—no one is to live for self.

The crazy thing was that Michael kept being accused of being selfish, and that is where many, deep down, had questions that were unanswered. Maybe he was selfish?

All were given one last chance, and as it is written in the Revelation, "There was war in heaven: Michael and his angels fought against the dragon; and the dragon fought and his angels, And prevailed not; neither was their place found any more in heaven. And the great dragon was cast out, that old serpent, called the Devil, and Satan, which deceives the whole world: he was cast out into the earth, and his angels were cast out with him."

You may think you've heard this story—I thought I had—but you haven't heard the half of it. I'm here to tell you how this war came to earth, how it involves humanity, and, according to all the oracles, how it's going to end.

EPISODE 2

THE MYSTERY

At first, Lucifer was in shock. Everyone was. Was Jannah supposed to carry on with business as usual? Each day seemed to have more questions than answers. With so much misunderstanding around the covenant, the citizens of Jannah, the guardians, were told that Lucifer would be given time to defend the principles he had shared.

Jannah felt empty. The family was torn apart. Just a few days later, reports started to circulate that earth and a new, distinct species was to be created—sentient beings with the ability to somehow create life; a race of beings almost as powerful as the guardians, yet with powers that even the guardians didn't have. We don't know if other civilizations out there have the power to procreate like we do, but we do know there was something unique about us.

Before immortality was granted to us, there was to be a test of loyalty.

After Lucifer and his followers were cast out, there was some kind of meeting, understanding, and agreement between Michael and Lucifer regarding the rules of engagement. The result of that meeting was an understanding that outlines intervention, protection, war, sickness, miracles, prayer, possession, oppression, abductions, visitations, violence, dreams, visions, prophecies, predictions, and more. There seems to be some sort of binding agreement by which both sides abide.

If mankind was to pass the test, they would become free to occupy the estates formerly enjoyed by Lucifer and the legions. The basis of freedom is choice. Mankind must enter the contest just like everyone else does: by choosing whom we will follow and serve.

You may be wondering if other sentient beings have had to take a similar test of loyalty. It seems so, but we on earth are the only ones to have chosen Lucifer.

Lucifer was no longer allowed in the city, so he would stand outside the gate, mock and taunt the guardians, and seek to shame them when they passed through. On one of these trips, a guardian was headed back to the city from an assignment. As you near the city, you can start to hear the music, smell the flowers ... and this time, this guardian was called over for a chat with Lucifer. He wanted a meeting with Michael. The guardian delivered the news, and Michael agreed and met with Lucifer.

Lucifer shared that he had made a mistake and wanted to come back. He would take any position assigned to him. The oracles who have seen this scene in vision describe how Michael began to weep. He told Lucifer it wasn't possible and that deep down, rebellion had taken root.

This was confusing to many of the guardians. For a long time, no one understood, but from that day on, Lucifer became relentless. Then the creation project began. Everyone was there to witness it. Elohim, the three beings we referred to earlier as the Administration, were there.

Michael led out. Each day was full of activity: the azure sky; turquoise waters; green forests. Then came the animals, whales, and birds. And then came humanity, made from the minerals, bacteria, particles, and nutrients of the ground, with all we needed to enjoy life forever.

However, that wasn't all. After all was created, a day was established as a holiday to be celebrated each week so that humans would never forget their origins and destiny—a sabbath of bliss on the seventh day of every week.

Once everything was completed, rumors began to spread from the legion camp. Misery loves company, right? Well, it wasn't long before they seemed to be up to something. They thought that if they could persuade mankind to join them, then maybe, just maybe, Elohim would let them back into the city, or, worst case, they would make earth their headquarters to show everyone what liberty and following your heart looked like.

Look around today; take a good look: this is what their regime has brought us. This is what following your heart looks like: selfishness to the Nth degree.

After we humans were created, the guardians would meet daily with our ancestors to share about the secrets of nature, the history of the war, and how to not be led astray.

Lucifer didn't come at them as a being of dazzling brightness. Instead, he possessed the most beautiful of all creation: the golden flying serpent that, at this time, was in appearance more like a dragon, large with wings, golden scales, and eyes like flames of fire. Mankind was 15 to 18 feet tall, and trees were thousands of feet tall, so this creature would have been massive and stunning.

Lucifer, now possessing this creature, would share the same message he did in Jannah. He shared with the woman that there were things being held back from her and her husband—mysteries—and happiness would only be found in following their own desires; their own hearts. Lucifer believed the covenant was an impossible idea and Jah was just being selfish.

This was primetime TV. Everyone was watching: the guardians, unfallen realms, everyone. The woman walked towards the tree of knowledge. She began to gaze upon it. You could almost hear in her countenance her asking the question, 'What was different about this tree? It looked similar to the tree of life.'

And just then, as if Lucifer was reading her thoughts, he asked her if Michael told her not to eat of every tree of the garden. She was enchanted with the idea of a creature that could communicate with her audibly. No other creature had done that yet. The serpent began to whisper how beautiful she was. It never crossed her mind that this could be the enemy about whom they had been warned.

Moment by moment, she began to wonder if what he was saying could be true. If the fruit of this tree led to this creature being able to talk, what could it do for her?

She was handed a piece of the fruit of this tree, and she ate it. She felt as though something magical was happening, so she grabbed more fruit and ran to her companion. She relayed the feelings she was having and the mystical powers of this fruit that caused animals to speak, but the father of our race knew, deep down, this was the enemy about whom they had been warned.

Everyone watching was in absolute disbelief. Jannah went silent. Mankind had chosen Lucifer as their leader. They would now be slaves to him.

Adam felt he couldn't live without this beautiful woman by his side. Eve did seem happier to him, and he decided to share her fate, whatever that may be. At first, they thought they felt better, enlightened, but once their robes of light began to disappear, there seemed to be a chill in the air. They both hid in shame, and Lucifer went off to celebrate.

The question on everyone's minds was, 'Would this event now give Lucifer and the legions entrance back into Jannah?'

If we had passed the test, we were to be given access to Jannah and all the realms, but once Lucifer took the title as king of the blue planet, he, with each leader of each planet, was granted access to the councils at the Capitol in Jannah. There is plenty of evidence in the Hebrew Scriptures of other intelligent life out there.

As everyone was trying to understand what had just happened, it was told that Michael and Jah were having a private meeting. Michael came out of the meeting three times with emotions all over the place. No one understood what was going on. Finally, Michael walked out and stated that they had a plan to save humanity and one day end the war and restore peace to all realms.

The accusation had been made that Jah and Michael were selfish dictators. They would refute that accusation. How? By Michael becoming one with mankind—becoming one of us and restoring us to the same condition as it was in the beginning. Michael shared that He would lay down all His powers, title, and authority, live as man, and be fully dependent on the intervention of the guardians to accomplish His mission.

Michael would never again have all the powers that He once did. His omnipresence (his ability to be anywhere and everywhere at once) would forever be gone. He would become one with the human race. Everything was at risk.

If Lucifer could lead Michael to betray the covenant and choose self over love, all would be lost. Mankind, through Michael, would prove to be faithful to the covenant, and through His sacrifice, could live again and eventually forever.

When Michael told the guardians that He would give up His life to save humanity, many offered to give up their lives instead but were told only the life of one of the Elohim would satisfy the accusations.

Before this, Michael had been visiting that first couple each day in the garden. Once this plan to save humanity was announced to all of Jannah and the unfallen realms, He went to inform mankind.

The couple was hiding in the garden when Michael got there, blaming each other. They were told they would have to leave this paradise, and death would be the result of their choice. They wept as they walked out with Michael's arms around them.

Once out of the garden, Michael revealed the plan to them. This mystery that had been hidden from all realms for ages. He told them there was hope. He would become one of them. He would take their penalty upon Himself. He would show that the covenant was the only way peace could be sustained and restored. He would have to lay down His life to save mankind.

They couldn't really grasp what He was saying, so He demonstrated in the most painful way: an innocent lamb was sacrificed, and a system was inaugurated to remind them of the awful results of selfishness and disregard of the covenant—ultimately, death. As awful as this sounds, without it, humanity would forget to what selfishness ultimately leads: extinction without a Savior.

This concept is hard to understand, but if you think about it, it's like two individuals, a man and a woman, being put on an island. They can work together, thrive, and make babies, or they can war against each other, hate each other, and eventually one will kill the other. Then, alone, the remaining being will ultimately get old and die, the end being extinction.

We've seen this experiment, this war, play out for thousands of years; and we see in nature and culture that we are constantly choosing between these two principles, selfishness and love.

Even today, our brightest minds recognize we need an intervention, or we will ultimately go extinct.

Because time must be given for both principles to play out, Lucifer began to realize his only way of escape was to get as many on this planet as possible to side with him. This meant he and the legions must replace Elohim in people's hearts to try and gain the victory. How he would do that is ... what we will find out next.

EPISODE 3

THE STORM

I hope what I'm sharing with you is making sense. What I'm going to tell you next will help connect some more dots. When the mystery was revealed, no one knew how long it would be.

After they left the garden, that first couple began to have children, but with greater access to the mind, Lucifer and the legions began disseminating their campaign to anyone who would listen. Eventually, one of those sons rose up and killed the other.

As more children were born, they would choose sides. One side believed liberty was only granted with self-control and self-government. The other believed that liberty was unfettered license, and to follow desire was the highest ambition. One lived to love others; the other lived to love self.

With each passing generation, it became clear that unless something drastic happened—unless there was an intervention—mankind would become extinct. The earth's ecosystems were collapsing, and it was hard to get anyone to see it. With humanity's appetite unchecked, what would prevent us from eating the animal kingdom into extinction? With humans living nearly 1,000 years, there was little to which they could not set their hearts, minds, and appetites.

The reason this sounds familiar is because we're witnessing similar scenes; the creation is crying out, and it seems no one is listening. We can only live so long for self, without any regard for others, until extinction is the result. There are only so many trees to cut down to grow food for animals that we will eat until a total collapse.

In those years after the garden, selfishness was rampant. Greed, lust, and violence were out of control. Mankind gloried in its works, things, accomplishments—itself! Violence increased daily. Selfishness became the norm. Anyone who even hinted at the covenant was hunted and destroyed, if possible. Marriage was no longer sacred. War was routine. Few remembered how the war began in Jannah.

More and more, the legions convinced humans that they were to become like the gods. There was no supreme god; all were gods accountable only to themselves. The legions and guardians were only permitted to intervene in the affairs of mankind when asked.

However, in the midst of all of this chaos, one man held onto hope. He lived in accordance with the covenant. He believed love and kindness were more sustainable than violence and selfishness. Finally, he was warned in a dream that without intervention, mankind would become extinct. He was warned of a coming climate catastrophe—a global storm.

You have to remember the entire earth was a tropical paradise; perfect climate everywhere. All life was watered from beneath. Humans had all they needed to live a long, healthy life. They could do anything to which they put their minds. Their civilizations and technology are believed to have been far advanced of any today. They began to venture into bioengineering, splicing DNA together (chimeras, animals for warfare), harvesting organs for immortality ... anything they could imagine, or at least thought they were imagining.

With abilities beyond our realm, the legions can instill thoughts and ideas into minds to the point where we are very prone to believe we are the originator of that concept or idea. In reality, in many cases, these ideas are being given by Lucifer and the legions. That's how it's always been and still is. This idea of gaining wisdom and knowledge from intelligent alien life is not a new concept. Humans from thousands of years ago were just as prone to the idea that if other life forms have been around longer than we have, then of course they know more than we do. If we are always progressing, then of course they are "light years" ahead of us.

However, there is a price for this wisdom: allegiance; devotion; worship; war; whatever is requested. The legion race is playing the long game, while we humans, with our finite minds, too often think of the short span of life on earth. It's really not fair.

For nearly a century, the guardians were teaching the architect of the craft, and with these revelations, he shared with anyone who would listen how they could escape the coming crisis.

This climate catastrophe, this cosmic storm, was like nothing our world or any world had ever seen.

Water from just beyond our atmosphere began to fall like rivers through the firmament. It shot up from the crust of the earth with equal pressure. The winds picked up, the waters began to rise, waves began to form, and then there was the shriek of a hurricane. People tied themselves to the largest animals in search of higher ground, hoping they would survive.

The guardians protected the craft that had been built, with the few survivors and animals who got on it. Those inside were filled with terror. All the realms watched in shock. Death was everywhere. How did this happen?

Only a small number were saved from the destruction, but the promised One, a coming Savior, who had the keys of life and death, was not in this small family. What was going on?

One of the sons of the chief builder had not been the most supportive of the whole endeavor. Though he was saved physically from the storm, the desires of his heart were fanned by the whispers of Lucifer himself.

He kept having this thought that Jah and Michael were unfair. Lucifer told him how mankind was on the verge of greatness before the storm. This son, who we know as Khawm, was separated from this small family, and he and his wife and son began to build an empire, with a tower at its center, that would, if possible allow them to escape earth and enter the realm of the gods.

They knew there was a secret that if they could just escape earth, they could seek to possibly colonize Jannah and attain to their divine calling, tearing Jah from the throne and taking what was rightfully theirs. The tower was unlike any structure ever built: 20 miles at the base. All of Khawm's descendants were required—forced actually—to help build this metropolis.

They were giants, believed to be 18 feet tall at this time. Lucifer was inspiring them at every step of the way. His legions assisted in the building. Their strength and wisdom made the feat of making a tower to pierce through the atmosphere seem possible. There is talk of space elevators today; this was a space staircase.

The guardians were told to go and confuse their language. The result led them to stop building the tower and spread out all over the earth. Without that, what was really going on was the building of a metropolis, with the desire for global domination by force, and ultimately Lucifer's attempt to recreate the city of Jannah on earth.

When men like Nimrod realized the guardians were actively engaged in the affairs of humanity, he and others began to yield their bodies and minds to the full possession and control of the legions. They would then build temples and offer sacrifices to these supposed gods. The humans would use hallucinogens that helped them completely turn off any ability to resist the possession of Lucifer and his followers.

Lucifer offered these men power, sex, wealth, and pleasure in exchange for devotion to his cause. However, people believed they were worshipping advanced beings from other realms or fallen war heroes with greater power than any human had yet attained. They didn't understand the full story ... yet.

When we hear reports of ancient visitors to this planet, like the Annunaki and other intelligent beings, could it be that these are just other names for this fallen race of beings from Jannah?

They would often change their names, but it seems to always be the same: the legions posing as gods under names like Baal, Ashtoreth, Zeus, Chemosh, Marduk, Milcom, Molech, Ra, Anubis ... all the gods of legend and myth.

They would tell people that they were fallen heroes of ages past or visitors from other realms and planets with advanced knowledge to which mankind had not yet attained. They would often appear as huge beings, far superior to humans in strength and knowledge, and reveal secrets of technology totally foreign to them.

With their understanding of the laws of nature, these beings could manipulate the weather, so you can see why mankind believed in the gods of thunder, rain, lightning, earth, sky, and sea. There are some writings of oracles in history that describe how these gods are going to return one day to the great cities of earth to perform the same apparent miracles. Some of them will masquerade as heroes of ages past or beings from other worlds, just like they always have.

Is there anything we've been told so that we are not deceived by this coming deception?

There is one idea that is almost universally accepted today that prepares the world for the arrival of these beings: the belief that the dead are not dead. Most people today believe that death is just a passing of the soul from this realm to another, and the souls of the dead can visit humanity and reveal secrets and mysteries to them.

There is no greater bond than love. It is the strongest of all emotions. We can't understand it, but only experience it. Lucifer knows of its power. It was his job to reveal this principle—the covenant—to all realms when he was the chief ambassador of Jannah. However, Lucifer, the light bearer, abandoned the covenant and twisted its meaning. He proudly promotes his policy and campaign slogan: license is liberty and love is desire.

Up until this climate catastrophe, the deluge, death had been a mystery. Most people just believed that when you died, it was over. Some believed there was hope, but they didn't really understand it. Lucifer capitalized on this, but even he didn't fully grasp it. He wasn't sure if death was eternal or if mankind would be recreated somehow, someway.

Regardless, he took matters into his own hands and began to have his legions make it appear as though relatives were coming back from the grave to reveal secrets hidden from mankind, when in reality it was just impersonations by Lucifer and his fallen followers. Slowly and gradually, the majority of mankind believed this to be true.

Is there any danger to this belief? For billions today, the idea of a loved one staring down or visiting from paradise is a thought that seems comforting. However, if death is just a door to the next life, then why sustain life? Why live in light of the covenant? Why love at all if you can just enjoy being selfish? If everyone lives on after death, what prevents the heart from doing whatever it wants in this life?

Get all you can out of this life, by whatever means you can, as much as you can, and then enjoy the next life when this life ends. Live however you want. Jannah is your home. That's the lie. That's Lucifer's campaign motto.

I remember when my dad died. It was like a part of me died. The worst part of death is wishing you had done things differently while that person lived. I recognize now that I took him for granted while he was alive. I remember that for months after, all I could do was dream about him. All I wanted to do was see him and just be with him one more time. That is how most feel with someone they love. They would do anything to see that person again.

I kept having these dreams that I could talk to him. It was so real. However, if we understand the teaching of death based on the Sacred Writings, then death is in reality like a sleep. They are at peace; not looking down on us; not coming back to visit us; and not being tortured in the flames of hell.

Nevertheless, that craving to be with them one more time is almost overwhelming. For many in the ancient world, they begged for it and went to mediums to talk to whom they thought were their dead relatives.

Let's be honest: that's not just the ancient world; we see it in pretty much everything Hollywood produces today.

There is this story of an ancient king. He had banished any communication with the dead from all the land. He knew it was just the fallen spirits masquerading as loved ones or visitors from other realms. Yet he craved an experience, an emotional high, that would satisfy his sorrow. Therefore, he goes to a witch (a necromancer, a medium) and pleads to talk to a friend who had recently died. He knows it's not his friend who is conjured up in this séance, but he doesn't care. He's thrown caution to the wind.

This is Lucifer's favorite method, and sadly nearly the whole world today believes this is all real: that we can communicate with those who have passed on. It's leading somewhere … somewhere terrifying. I will tell you more on that later.

The legions are highly organized. They have specialties in evoking emotions in mankind like strife, intemperance, unkindness, selfishness, greed, jealousy, passion, ambition, competition, appetite, lust, and hatred. Thankfully, the guardians have specialties too.

We clearly aren't alone. We are in the middle of a war bigger than ourselves. And what the legions couldn't do, Lucifer decided he would do himself through a one-on-one battle with the Prince of the Covenant. There is more on that in our next episode.

EPISODE 4

The Desert

Watt I'm about to tell you is perhaps the most divisive subject in world history. It's the event we track time with; it's the event that sparked a global revolution and forever changed the power structures. It all started in the desert of Palestine nearly 2,000 years ago. The sun was bright; the sky was blue; the desert nomad had been warning about something ominous yet revolutionary on the edge of the desert. At this time, Israel was the cultural crossroads for the entire world, so news traveled fast.

Many believed Israel was soon to be rid of the Roman yoke and again regain global dominance. All they needed was the power that once was theirs—that mystical, supernatural force that annihilated armies in a night; that force that dwelt in the golden box they carried into war—or so they thought. The Messiah was the last piece of the puzzle of global dominance.

The nation of Israel was looking for a king to conquer the nations; someone to command the armies with invincibility. Instead, a poor, Galilean child from Nazareth was rumored to be the Chosen One, but he didn't look the part. And as soon as the desert prophet boldly claimed Yeshua was the One for whom they had hoped, Lucifer feared for the safety of his kingdom.

Lucifer had remembered a prophecy Michael gave way back in the garden: one day, a child would be born who would crush the head of the serpent; and Lucifer fully understood who was represented by the serpent.

As Yeshua stepped out of the Jordan River, He was not headed to the City of David to be crowned king by the crowds like they hoped, but instead He headed to the desert ... by Himself!

Israel expected this moment for thousands of years—that a king would come to make war—but this was because of a misunderstanding of the prophecies. Selfishness, empire building, and ambition led them to misunderstand the writings of the seers and oracles of old that foretold of the mystery being revealed: One like a lamb, humble, innocent, going to the slaughter.

The time had come—a date with destiny. If mankind was to be saved from destruction, One of mankind would have to pass the test given in the garden, but not in the mind and body of a man like Adam, a giant with no temptations, sins, or inherited tendencies; no, this time it would be after 4,000 years of a degenerated race. After thousands of years of selfishness had nearly destroyed humanity, Issa al Masih, the Messiah, the Prince, Yeshua, Jesus, whatever name you choose to call Him, would endure the threefold test under the direst circumstances. He would overcome where mankind had fallen. He would take the crown from Lucifer and forever secure it on humanity.

Thirty years earlier, Michael, the prince of Jannah, stepped down and became one with mankind. The son of Mary, He grew up as a man and now would enter upon the very reason for His existence: a mysterious purpose, to save mankind, reveal the mystery to all realms, and begin to put an end to all the lies said about Him and Jah.

For thousands of years, mothers and fathers had relayed to their children the story that one day, the Prince would come and save them from the destruction of selfishness before it was too late. When the Spanish fleet landed on the shores of the New World, Cortez turned to them and said, "Burn the ships." That moment, 30 years prior in Bethlehem, was the same; there was no going back. Everything depended on Him. Everything in the universe was at risk!

When Jerusalem was destroyed the first time by the Babylonian Empire, one of the Hebrew slaves was visited by a guardian and given visions and dreams of the future. He foretold of this event when the Prince would come. With that said, you need to know the condition of the world at this time.

The world was under one government; most spoke one common language; everyone was enamored with entertainment, pleasure, and sports; the people were tired of religion and the dryness of it all. They wanted something fresh; something that would give them hope; something that was genuine.

Israel was pretty much universally deceived and deluded by the demon of ambition. Roman rule was all about which they could think. When this Galilean was born, rumors began to circulate of a coming Deliverer who would establish a kingdom solely for the chosen race and from which would be excluded every other people on the earth. It was believed that the Messiah would break the heathen yoke, lift up His people, and designate princes among them. All nations would be summoned to appear before the One sent by Jah and would called upon to surrender themselves or be consumed.

As you can see, this is not the same picture of a being who came to save His creation by voluntarily sacrificing Himself for them.

Lucifer watched as the Prince came up out of that desert river. He watched Him walk into the wilderness and followed Him. At first, he wasn't clear on what was going on. He had heard the voice from the sky. This was confirmation that this was the One. As he followed this weak-looking Palestinian into the desert, he couldn't understand why Michael would have left the city of Jannah and become one with this degraded species of humanity. It filled him with fear and anxiety that his days were numbered and his power would be broken. He knew what the seers had foretold and that everything was dependent on this moment—that the fullness of time had come.

The book of Hebrews tells us, "For this reason he had to be made like mankind, fully human in every way, in order that he might become a merciful and faithful high priest in service to Jah, and that he might make atonement. Because he himself suffered when he was tempted, he is able to help those who are being tempted."

Many think Michael, now Yeshua, was some superhero acting a part, which totally downplays what really happened. Michael had laid down all powers and became a weak human with the ability to access power from Jannah, just like any other human could.

Here were the three tests the Man must pass: the lust of the flesh, the lust of the eyes, and the pride of life—all three where mankind had fallen in the beginning. However, once into the desert, everything started to change. Even the facial expressions of Yeshua began to change, like a great burden was laid upon Him. For 40 days, He didn't eat or drink. He looked like He was dying. And then finally, the time came.

Lucifer hadn't been seen for many days, but then out of the blue sky he appeared like a flash of lightning. He was beautiful, young, vibrant, and full of wisdom.

Words don't do him justice. He began to walk up to the Prince, appearing as a guardian from Jannah. He stated that he had been sent as a kind gesture to sympathize with Him. He said, "Jah doesn't require such excruciating self-denial and suffering. I have come from the city of Jannah to tell you that you were only asked to prove your **willingness** to endure, and you have passed the test. Congratulations are in order. You don't need to continue to suffer painful hunger and death from starvation. Let me help you."

This dude is one smooth mamma jamma.

But it gets better. Lucifer then says, "I'm trying to be generous here, considering the circumstances. I know that for many years, your mother misled you into thinking you were someone special. After the adultery, your stepdad Joseph tried to cover it up and had your mother believe this fanciful fantasy. Look at you. Look around. Did they not tell you? Allow me: One of the most exalted Guardians of Jannah has been exiled to the earth. ... Yeshua, you should know that you are no prince of Jannah, but instead a traitor. You are the fallen Lucifer who has been banished. Look at our appearances—the evidence is clear."

This was a masterclass in psychological warfare.

Lucifer went on to say that it was not in the character of Jah to permit anyone to endure such extreme suffering like this unless, of course, in the event that Yeshua was actually the archenemy of Jannah. Then, perhaps, conditions were right.

Lucifer was hoping to plant and insinuate just enough doubt to get the Prince to assert Himself, because if Yeshua used any of His powers to which he had access, then He could not honestly stand in the place of humanity as a human.

Lucifer went on to state that Yeshua was clearly no representative of Jannah, much less a commander in the royal courts. Yeshua's appearance indicated that He was clearly forsaken by His own race and the realm of Jannah. However, if He wanted to prove Himself, then just a simple test could be demonstrated by taking the stone at His feet and turning it into some bread; nothing fancy, just bread. If He could do this— work magic for His own benefit —then Lucifer would give Him the benefit of the doubt.

How does Yeshua respond to all of this? He acted like He hadn't heard a word. He came to save the race, not Himself. That was the accusation in the capitol eons before: that He was just out for Himself. Of everything in the garden, remember the test was appetite. Mankind could eat everything except the fruit of one tree. Adam wasn't even hungry when he faced his test. The Prince hasn't had food for 40 days in the hot desert sun. He responds with the words, "Man doesn't live by bread alone, but by every word out of the mouth of Jah."

This was the first test. There are two more.

Lucifer wanted to make sure Yeshua knew of his superior strength, so he carried Him into Jerusalem, set Him on the pinnacle of the temple, and said, "If truly you are who you say you are, throw yourself down from here."

You see, the first temptation with bread was about making Yeshua doubt that Jah cared for Him. This temptation was to lead Yeshua into presumption. Lucifer thought misquoting some Scripture would confuse Him, but Yeshua knew what was going on and said, "It is written, don't tempt Jah!"

Lucifer was, in essence, trying to get Yeshua to commit suicide and end this war once and for all.

However, what few realize is that Lucifer was trying to practice hypnotism and telepathy on Yeshua, but it wasn't working. Remember, in both of these temptations, it was this young, commanding, beautiful being presenting himself as an ambassador of Jannah, contrasted with this emaciated Palestinian at the door of death, but then it all changed. After Lucifer realized this wasn't working, he changed his tactics. Now he removed the disguise.

He then takes Yeshua up on this mountain, of which few know the location and which has a view of the whole earth. Lucifer then describes how he has become the prince of all the earth—all the kingdoms. He reveals the glory of all the kingdoms off in the distance, and Yeshua can only **see** the glory of them. This was the most powerful of all temptations. There is nothing to which Yeshua looked forward more than when the earth is teeming with a new civilization and buzzing with activity, untainted by selfishness.

Lucifer showed Yeshua the glory of these kingdoms and said that he was willing to hand over the dominion thereof to Him as a gift—no fight, no suffering, no sorrow. The scepter held by Lucifer over all the earth would be given to the Prince in exchange for one small gesture: bow down, worship Lucifer, and honor him as His superior, the benevolent benefactor.

For a moment, Yeshua looked out but he knew all would be lost. He turned away, looked straight into the piercing eyes of Lucifer, and said, "Get away from me. It is written, 'Worship Jah and serve Him only!'" He then fell on the ground, nearly dead. Lucifer left. A unit of guardians was sent to encourage Him, prepare some food for Him, eat with Him, and celebrate the victory!

You would think that the war would now be over, but not yet, because that was only one victory of many that had to be won. The next was back in Jerusalem. The Hebrews had long-expected a conquering commander. Yeshua was not who they expected. He spends time with the poor, sick, and outcasts. He doesn't play to the politicians or religious leaders. He has a group of young men who start following Him.

After three-and-a-half years, He walks into the Garden of Gethsemane, unsure if He would survive the night from the turmoil and burden He was carrying. Lucifer was there too; he wasn't going to miss this.

The war began long before with Lucifer accusing Yeshua (then called Michael) of being selfish and holding things back from the citizens of Jannah and other worlds. Now, the contest would be decided. Lucifer had been preparing for this moment. Everything was at stake here. If either one failed here, all was lost for his rule.

Yeshua had proved in His life, especially in the desert, that mankind could live an unselfish life. He had won the crown as Prince of the earth, but still, mankind was lost and without hope of immortality without an intervention. Yeshua would prove that Jah and He were not selfish like they were accused of being. Thus, the destiny of mankind and all created beings—the very existence of Jannah—was all weighing in the balance this night.

Knowing all that, what do you think Lucifer would do to make one last attempt at a victory? He can't kill Yeshua, so he has to lead Him outside the protection of Jah and the guardians, and to do that, Lucifer began whispering that if Yeshua lays down His life for mankind, the separation from Jannah and Jah would be eternal. He whispered, "What would be gained from this sacrifice anyway? Look at how ungrateful humanity was!"

All these thoughts are being implanted "telepathically" so that Yeshua had to filter each and every one to determine if they were His own or from the archenemy. Lucifer cast doubts by saying, "The people who claim to be above all others in temporal and spiritual advantages have rejected You. They are seeking to destroy You, the Foundation, Center, and Seal of the promises made to them as a peculiar people. All will forsake You!"

Yeshua's whole being shuddered. The conflict was terrible. The guilt of a world lying in the darkness of selfishness and superstition pressed upon Him. All the unfallen worlds were watching this moment; all the citizens of Jannah; everyone.

Yeshua's body was dying. His heart would not survive the stress. It began to come apart. He began to sweat drops of blood. He was praying for a way of escape. In this moment, He believes He will forever be cut off from his family—from Jah—because sin and selfishness are so destructive. Nevertheless, He finally sees no other way and fully commits to complete the mission, no matter what, thoroughly believing He would not make it through the tomb; but others would, and that made it worth it! This is the essence of love. He didn't have to do this, but He chose to lay down His life. All pagan religions and their dieties require sacrifice from humanity. This story is different.

The prophecy of this night described how Yeshua would willingly go as a lamb to the slaughter. All must see the extent to which people and fallen angels would go to destroy the Life-giver. Crowds inspired by these demons mocked Him. Nothing could stop His march to free the captives. The last temptation was a line hurled from the mob whispered in their ears by the legion of demons on the ground: "Save Yourself!

Others you saved, so save yourself." However, this was what the war was all about: selfishness or selflessness. He chose love—love for people that didn't understand it.

It makes you ask, 'Why He would go through with this for people like them? like me?' Because the foundation of His government is love—complete unselfishness. Everyone watched the moment He shouted victoriously, "It was finished!"

Notwithstanding, we are told that many of the guardians still wondered, in these last few scenes, if perhaps there hadn't been just a big misunderstanding, but now, they finally saw Lucifer unmasked. He had clothed himself in such a beautiful disguise that many didn't fully comprehend what his administration and campaign were all about.

This day, love and selfishness stood face to face, and love won! You could hear the celebration through all the worlds that the mission had been accomplished. The Administration of Jannah was clearly innocent, and Lucifer and his followers were the guilty parties with false accusations.

Nevertheless, there were still some unanswered questions. Some of the guardians still need clarification, and for the sake of mankind, the contest was allowed to continue. Yeshua promised He would return one day in the future, but the mystery had a few more secrets to it.

EPISODE 5

My Confession

Imagine screaming sounds, crackling of fire, and a lions roar. You never really get those sounds out of your mind, especially when you know what they are. Those are the sounds of our ancestors: boys, girls, moms, dads, brothers, sisters, grandparents, and friends—people who stood for principle while others, under the influence of the legions of demons, carried out the agenda of Lucifer, all under the name of the Christian church and the sign of the cross.

The prophecies had said Yeshua would rise on the third day. As was foretold, His followers found the tomb empty on that morning. He then went to the Capitol in Jannah. Everyone was celebrating as Yeshua entered, but He was preoccupied, not celebrating.

He was focused on something. He went straight into the temple—straight to Jah. He wanted to make sure all had been satisfied. Once He came out, He released a shout of victory that echoed throughout the galaxy.

Many religious persons have shared parts of the story I've been sharing with you throughout the world, but most haven't shared the whole story. Many don't like this part of the story.

This was a revolutionary moment. The Messiah's teachings instructed people to turn the other cheek, don't cheat others, and treat others like they would want to be treated. However, once Lucifer knew the battle was lost, the battle was on. Nearly 40 years later, the city of peace, Jerusalem—thought to be the eternal city—was burned to the ground. In just a few decades, all of Yeshua's closest friends, His disciples, had been charged with treason and executed in countries around the world, but one—just one—survived. Finally, they sentenced him to an island prison in the Mediterranean: Patmos. His name was John.

They tried to kill him—boil him alive, burn him alive, and other attempts—but were unsuccessful. He was chosen to write some of the most shocking words in history: 22 pages in the book called the Revelation, which would become more relevant with each passing century. The Prince came to visit him and reveal to him what would take place in the future. He was shown by one of the guardians the future all the way down to our day and beyond. He was shown the judgment of Babylon the Great, this global, fraudulent system that has done so much damage on the earth, with whom the kings of the earth have "committed fornication." John calls her a whore and says, "The inhabitants of the earth were made drunk with the wine of her fornication."

Those are not my words; that's how John writes it; but in our vernacular, John saw a system; an empire of selfishness and greed that would become worldwide; a system that puts desire, money, and profits above principle, people, and need. John wrote how the teachings of Yeshua would be hijacked and state-run. He saw the same sequence of empires that the seer Daniel had been shown in vision many years before. The rise and fall of the empires of Ancient Babylon, Persia, Greece, Rome, and then ...

Well, then Lucifer changed his methods. Saint Peter, as they call him, the very one upon whom the universal church was said to be founded, made a rather provocative statement: He called the eternal city, Rome, "Babylon." John wrote how the universal Christian church would become the greatest enemy of honest followers of Yeshua.

You heard me right. He wrote how the Christian church would become the greatest enemy of the followers of Yeshua.

Constantine sees this schism that the Christians and pagans had. He has this epiphany, this vision in battle, and does his best to merge these two diverse belief systems. Just as the seer Daniel had seen nearly 1,000 years before, this persecuting power, under the guise of the Christian church—this hybrid of religion and government—would begin to change laws, calendars, holidays, and holy days. However, that was just the beginning; it got much worse.

Those who wanted to keep the principles that the Prince had taught were persecuted and hunted like wild animals. They began to live in the mountains for fear of capture and torture. They wanted freedom of conscience at any cost. Deep down, we all desire the freedom to follow the dictates of our own consciences.

The celebration of the weekly holiday of creation on the seventh day was one of their identifying marks. They were called the Waldenses, Albigenses, Huguenots, etc., but they could not endure the hatred that existed in the cities of the Old World, so they moved to the countryside and remote places in the mountains to try to enjoy life. They wanted to worship the Creator while the pagans enjoyed worshipping the creation, but the falling away from truth and love began the downfall of the Old World.

History tells us this lasted for over 1,400 years. That's why our history books refer to it as the "Dark Ages." People hated the light and did all they could to shroud everything in mystery and darkness. They burned, tortured, and imprisoned those who didn't fall in line with the religion of the state. Babylon the Great, the power about which John was warned, ruled the world and built its empire and wealth on the backs of its poor, ignorant citizens.

Take St. Peter's Basilica: Do you know how it was funded? By salesmen on behalf of the church who would go around into cities and villages and sell certificates of indulgence. These indulgences were, in essence, licenses to commit any crime imaginable. They were said to forgive any sins one had committed. They also could be used to reduce the torture of loved ones in the flames of hell, but in order to make so many people want to buy these, they had to preach the fear of hell and the fire that tortures its inhabitants.

To any student of the words of scripture and Yeshua, hell is an event, not a place where people are burning.

The so-called Christian church has claimed authority that is not hers. Her priests claim the ability to forgive sin. This is what the Scriptures identify as blasphemy.

To control people, you usually just need to put fear into them. The idea, perpetuated for thousands of years, of a divine being torturing bad people was just the marketing campaign for global control.

Will fire be used to destroy those who hate Jah, Jannah, and all for which it stands? In an event, one time, for a moment, we are told, "Yes," but that fire is kindled specifically for that hideous monster called Babylon. The prophecies of Daniel foretold that this symbol, the eternal city, would in fact not be eternal but rule for only 1,260 years, until the year 1798. Nevertheless, even before that time ended, the rays of hope began to shine on the world.

Truth is rarely popular, especially with those in power. One of the prophecies had foretold a proposed change in the very laws of Jannah, the same given on Sinai thousands of years before. The universal Christian church claimed to have authority to change these, but she was never given this power or authority. Yeshua made it clear He did not come to destroy the law, but to fulfill it. This new system was just a way to blend the worship of the Creator with the pagan worship of nature.

The church removed the commandment to not bow down to idols. With that said, the biggest change she claimed to make was that the first day of the week, the weekly holiday of the empire, the day of the sun, was the day for worship, not the seventh day, as it had been for millennia. This is what the Scriptures call the "wine" (a symbol of lies) of Babylon.

Around this time, Columbus is said to be on his voyage looking for the New World. The Light of Jannah is being printed by Gutenberg and others and read by more and more. Around this time, a devout priest, Martin Luther, takes a journey to Rome. He is about to enter the city, falls to the earth, and says, "Holy Rome, I salute thee!" Upon exiting the city, he writes, "No one can imagine what sins are committed in Rome. ... If there is a hell, Rome is built over it!" On October 31, 1517, he posts 95 concerns he has with the abuses of the church.

However, since the church and state are united, he is really picking a fight with the empire. Now you know why this was so risky. Immediately, his life was threatened. Just like the revolutionary teachings of Yeshua nearly 1,500 years prior, the same concept—that anyone can escape the earth and be saved before it's too late—the very thing from which the sale of indulgences was profiting—was now beginning to be offered freely by people like Luther, who is teaching from Scripture that mankind can access Jah directly, rather than having to go through an intermediary. This marks the beginning of the protest against the dangers of mingling church and state. Thus, the Protestant Reformation begins!

As soon as the Reformation began, a counter-reformation began. The Society of Jesus, the Jesuit order, was initiated around this time to counter the influence and effects of Luther and the protestors.

"The Society of Jesus was and is the most cruel, unscrupulous, and powerful of all the champions of the universal Christian church ... To combat the Protestants, Jesuitism inspired its followers with a fanaticism that enabled them to endure like dangers, and to oppose to the power of truth all the weapons of deception. There was no crime too great for them to commit, no deception too base for them to practice, no disguise too difficult for them to assume. Vowed to perpetual poverty and humility, it was their studied aim to secure wealth and power, to be devoted to the overthrow of Protestantism, and the re-establishment of the papal supremacy.

It was a fundamental principle of the order that the end justifies the means. By this code, lying, theft, perjury, and assassination were not only pardonable but commendable, when they served the interests of the church. Under various disguises, the Jesuits worked their way into offices of state, climbing up to be the counselors of kings and shaping the policy of nations. They became servants to act as spies upon their masters; they established colleges for the sons of princes and nobles and schools for the common people; and the children of Protestant parents were drawn into an observance of the rites of the universal church."

Jah would see to it that freedom of conscience would not become extinct, and the New World was the only hope.

Episode 6

The New World

The Old World had continued long enough. It was time for something new. Hope was rising in the West. The New World, as it was called, was full of opportunities and possibilities, but more than anything, it was full of the promise of a better life—a life where people could follow the dictates of their own consciences. Around this time, the King of England, speaking of those who prized conscience over anything else, is quoted as saying, "Conform, or ... harry them out of the land, or else worse."

The New world was a land with no pope or king. Just as America was rising, the Old World was in the midst of the Revolution, in the heart of where the Inquisition had been the strongest: France. The year is 1798: the pope has been taken captive; the wealth gap has reached a climax between the haves and the have-nots. That's often what happens in revolution: once people have nothing left to lose, they lose it. You can hear the rumblings of this today. Nevertheless, this was no random moment; the period of time, long-foretold as 1,260 years of reign for the Old World and Rome, was over.

As the Old World was falling, the New World was rising, but many times, it's easier to take someone out of Babylon than to take Babylon out of someone. As those men and women boarded the boats headed for the New World, they longed for freedom, but as soon as they arrived, sadly they drove out the natives by violence.

Somehow, we often resort to force with others when they don't act like we think they should. This is not right. As those men, women, boys, and girls were boarding ships in Holland to sail to the shores of the New World, they listened to John Robinson, who told them that the Reformation, the protest against the mingling of church and state, must continue and not stall. He said if the great people who had raised up the torch were still around, they would keep looking for more light. He challenged them to never become satisfied with thinking they know enough.

Robinson is quoted as saying, "Remember your promise and covenant with Providence ... to receive whatever light and truth shall be made known to you from His written word ... for it is not possible the Christian world should come so lately out of such thick Anti-Christian darkness and that full perfection of knowledge should break forth at once."

They were unafraid to risk everything to escape the Old World and kiss the shores of the New World. As they boarded the ship, Robinson said to them, "I am very confident the Lord has more truth and light yet to break forth out of His holy word."

However, sadly, not long after they arrived, many began to mandate that only church members can serve in government, and it was not long before persecution arose ... in the New World. Nevertheless, hope had not disappeared. Another re-former rises up: Roger Williams; but even when Williams arrived in America, he found church attendance was mandated by law.

Williams was respected and loved as a faithful leader and minister; a man of rare gifts. Integrity and kindness were shown to everyone he met, but as he kept teaching and preaching tolerance and freedom of speech and conscience, he was accused of "subverting the government and society."

He was sentenced for a crime as an enemy of the state. To escape arrest, he was forced to flee, in the cold stormy winds of winter, into the deep forest. He later wrote, "For fourteen weeks, I was sorely tossed in a bitter season, not knowing what bread or bed did mean - but the ravens fed me in the wilderness and a hollow tree served as a shelter."

He continued through the snow and forest until he found refuge with an Indian tribe, whose confidence and affection he won while teaching them the truths from Jannah.

Finally, he made it to the shores of Narragansett Bay, where he laid the foundation for the first state in the New World that would recognize the essence of true freedom: "that every man should have the liberty to worship according to the light of his own conscience."

He established civil government on the doctrine of the liberty of conscience, the equality of opinions before the law. That state that he founded would become known as Rhode Island, and it became the asylum for civil and religious liberty—the cornerstones of the American Republic.

The Declaration of Independence says, "All men are created equal; that they are endowed by their Creator with certain unalienable rights; that among these are life, liberty, and the pursuit of happiness." And the Constitution guarantees, in the most explicit terms, the inviolability of conscience: "No religious test shall ever be required as a qualification to any office or public trust under the United States." And then perhaps most important line in it: "Congress shall make no law respecting an establishment of religion, or prohibiting the free exercise thereof."

Word gets out in the Old World, and thousands begin to risk their lives to escape to the New World. Most nations in history arose in turmoil; they must conquer or be conquered, and one by one, empires rise and fall. However, America was very different.

John, on the island of Patmos, saw America's rise, wrote that it would come up from the earth, and described it as unlike all the other ferocious beasts in the prophecies (lion, bear, leopard, dragon, etc.). Instead of a monster, John describes this new empire like an innocent lamb, the very symbol of Yeshua, and "like a silent seed planted in the earth, we grew into an empire."

The lamb in John's vision is described as having two horns—two symbols of its power: separation of church and state—a church without a pope; a state without a king; a republic self-governed by its own citizens. However, the scene changes, and John describes the lamb speaking like a dragon, the symbol of Lucifer.

Not all was a bed of roses. Already, the Puritan faith in the colonies seems to be turning into the persecution of the Dark Ages, and many once again lose any hope in the future. Then a war breaks out in 1812, and one man, a patriot in the army, wants nothing to do with religion. He sees how awful it has become, and it disgusts him. His name is William Miller.

He begins, almost for sport, to mock the Christian religion and such erroneous teachings like burning hell fire for bad people—God torturing people for all eternity. He mocked the rising teaching of a secret rapture, which opposed a visible second coming. He denounced the ideas that the dead moved on to the next life, prophecy was sealed, and God and the Bible were a mystery.

He saw no evidence that the millennium was to be on earth rather than not in heaven. Another teaching that Miller mocked was one that has, in reality, no basis in Scripture: Israel was the country to which to look in prophecy, rather than the United States. Miller saw none of these as having validity, but what intrigued him the most was the idea that the Bible could predict the future.

This man, who hated religion, ventured out to show how ridiculous the Bible was and how much it contradicted itself. He was also curious as to why he heard some scholars pronounce a curse on all who studied the ninth chapter of the book of Daniel, which foretold of a Promised Deliverer.

As he kept studying, he kept making more sense, rather than less, of the words he read. Finally, around the age of 34, he became convicted that the war that started long ago in Jannah was soon coming to an end; that a prophecy of 2,300 years was to end around 1844, which seemed to mark the end of all things.

A wealthy farmer, he was so convicted on this that he sold everything and went on the road, teaching anyone who would listen about what he had learned, but as the message of the end of the war was ramping up, a power from beneath was working to bring about the last great scenes in the drama—a power hoping to rip the nation in two to divide and conquer.

Guess who rejected Miller's teachings, that the end was near, the most: The Christians!

Most still had that old-world mentality rooted deep in the fibers of their being. "Many wanted to follow what they knew to be right but they trusted their pastors and priests who forbade them and others from listening to any proposed 'new light.'"

This was a great awakening in America and around the world. Many couldn't endure the persecution they would get from family and fellow church members, so they remained in deliberate ignorance in hopes of keeping the peace, but Yeshua said he did not come to bring peace, but instead to make people decide on which side of the war they were.

One of those who began to listen and follow Miller later stated, "He who deliberately stifles his convictions of duty because it interferes with his inclinations will finally lose the power to distinguish between truth and error."

Thomas Guthrie, a Presbyterian minister, began to write on the separation of Protestant churches: "300 years ago, our church, with an open Bible on her banner, and this motto 'Search the Scriptures' on her scroll, marched out from the gates of Rome ... But did they come clean out of Babylon?"

"The Church of England," said Charles Spurgeon," seems to be eaten through and through with sacramentarianism ... Those of whom we thought better things are turning aside one by one from the fundamentals of the faith ... I believe, the very heart of England is honeycombed with a damnable infidelity which dares still go into the pulpit and call itself Christian."

They lost sight of that glorious concept of truth: that it is always progressive.

When the church loses its power, it turns to power. Actually, when the church loses its power, it turns to force. When the church loses its supposed power from God, it turns to the power of mankind. And that's how a war would break out on American soil.

Episode 7

Divide and Conquer

I want you to really understand the emotions that so many were experiencing. Miller, the farmer-turned-preacher, on one of his speaking engagements, catches the attention of a young girl named Ellen Harmon.

The guardians had attempted to give insight into what the future held to two other men, but those men had refused to share what they had been shown, so the guardians began to give this girl dreams and visions and show her what was coming on the nation because of the rejection of the light.

The idea of humans receiving visions and dreams seems like an ancient concept. The seers and prophets of antiquity came at pivotal moments in the history of nations.

Miller, Harmon, and others began to share their hope that the end of this long controversy was near. Scores of people who called themselves Christians were rejecting the message, but they weren't just rejecting the idea of the hope of the return of Yeshua; they were rejecting other light that was flooding onto the scene: The idea that a God who tortures people in hellfire was and is not found in Scripture. The Scriptures are clear that the dead sleep rather than pass on into paradise and communicate with the living.

Many people rejected the truth that the weekly holy day was actually the seventh day, rather than the first day. The very things the Scriptures foretold would happen were now coming to pass, and Christians had no protection from this last deception of Lucifer and his legions.

Just for context, at this time in the mid-1800s, it seemed more likely that spiritualism would become the religion of America, compared to Christianity becoming the religion of the Roman Empire (in AD 156) or Islam becoming the religion of the Arabian peninsula (in AD 756). Most people today think the United States is primarily Christian, but if we really pinned down the belief systems of millions, we might more easily label them as adherents of spiritualism, the religion of Lucifer.

When you reject light, the doors of the soul are flung open to darkness. Everyone was rejecting the teachings of the Scriptures, so they naturally wanted to believe that their loved ones were happily living in Jannah and the living could communicate with these spirits of ancestors and departed loved ones at will.

The country was increasingly divided on the issue of slavery. The day was July 4, 1850: President Zachary Taylor is not as friendly to the southern states and their desire for the expansion of slavery. History says that he comes home from a nice holiday and eats a bowl of cherries. He's dead a few days later.

Suspicions are swirling that Jesuits had taken an oath to subvert the U.S. Constitution, and many believed they were behind Millard Filmore. Soon after this, Filmore became president and quickly moved through Congress everything against which Taylor had stood. In September, The Fugitive Slave Act is voted and strengthened.

Just for context, in this moment in history, there are more people who are communing with the dead (spiritualists) than who are against the abolition of slavery.

The Fugitive Slave Act was a law that stated that any slave who escaped to a northern state was by law to be returned to his or her slave master. By the North complying, they were aiding and abetting slavery. The law resulted in the kidnapping of free blacks and conscription into slavery.

They had no rights or defense in court, so they were, in essence, being hunted. This made things worse. Northern businessmen supported the law because they had strong financial ties with slave owners in the south.

It would be fair for us to ask where Jah was in all of this. Where were the guardians? Or where were the faithful—those who followed the teachings of Yeshua?

As the tensions rose, Ellen, the young girl getting these visions from the guardians, now married, was standing in front of a group of church parishioners on a cold winter's day in Parkville, Michigan on January 12, 1861. It would be just three months later when the first shot of the Civil War was fired at Fort Sumter.

The guardians showed her in vision what was soon to take place in the country. Here is what she said that day:

> There is not a person in this house who has even dreamed of the trouble that is coming upon this land. People are making sport of the secession ordinance of South Carolina, but I have just been shown that a large number of States are going to join that State, and there will be a most terrible war. In this vision I have seen large armies of both sides gathered on the field of battle. I heard the booming of the cannon, and saw the dead and dying on every hand. Then I saw them rush-

ing up engaged in hand-to-hand fighting [bayoneting one another]. Then I saw the field after the battle, all covered with the dead and dying. Then I was carried to prison, and saw the suffering of those in want, who were wasting away. Then I was taken to the homes of those who had lost husbands, sons, or brothers in the war. I saw there [sic] distress and anguish. ...

There are those in this house who will lose sons in that war.

As with most warnings, few listened, but some did. The Underground Railroad was at a peak. The guardians were helping men, women, boys, and girls escape the evils of the plantations. The wars the guardians fight, which we can't see, is as real as the ones that we can see.

It wasn't just Ellen with whom the guardians were working. You don't develop the courage and resolve of President Abraham Lincoln overnight. The guardians had been planting seeds within him throughout his whole life, all for this moment. This nation had yet to achieve her divine calling.

While Miller, Ellen, and others were sharing what was being shown to them, other guardians were working on using Lincoln as well. The preferred method is always to work through sincere followers of light, but there are times when the leader of a nation can do more in a moment than a common person can in a lifetime. The guardians tried to help Lincoln see what was really going on. They saw this scene long before: the same tactics to divide and conquer, led by Lucifer in the city of Jannah.

The temptations in Lincoln's life were many. His wife was a quintessential example. As with any mother who loses a child, Mary Lincoln was overwhelmed with grief, but rather than hold on to hope and follow the light, she went looking in the darkness. She loved to communicate with the dead. At this time, as the war broke out and the casualties began piling up, you can understand why it is in times of mass casualty that the desire to speak to the dead is the greatest.

Another factor of which few know is that the legions of fallen angels from Jannah were revealing themselves to the generals on both sides of the war, appearing as the spirits of their friends, dead warriors, and the fathers of the Revolutionary War. These generals were seeking counsel from the dead on how to wage war.

Lincoln did attend a few seances with his wife, but he was suspicious of it all. His calling was too great, and thankfully he didn't lose his way. Lincoln stayed in contact with a friend, a priest, and they were very open with each other. Here is an excerpt from one of those letters from Lincoln, dated June 8, 1864:

> Dear Friend, This war would never have been possible without the sinister influence of the Jesuits. We owe it to Popery that we now see our land reddened with the blood of her noblest sons....It is the promises of the Jesuits... the money and the arms...

> The Protestants of both the North and South would surely unite to exterminate the Jesuits if they could hear the plots made in Rome to destroy this Republic.

> Unfortunately, I feel more and more, every day, that it is not against the Americans of the South, alone, I am fighting, it is more against the Pope of Rome, his perfidious Jesuits [and their blind and blood-thirsty slaves,] than against the real American Protestants, that we have to defend ourselves.

> Here is the real danger of our position. So long as they will hope to conquer the North, they will spare me; but the day we will rout their armies (and that day will surely come, with the help of God), take their cities, and force them to submit, then, it is my impression that the Jesuits, who are the principal rulers of the South, will do what they have almost invariably done in the past. The dagger, or the pistol of one of their adepts, will do what the strong hands of the warriors could not achieve.

This civil war seems to be nothing but a political affair to those who do not see, as I do, the secret springs of that terrible drama. But it is more a religious than a civil war. It is Rome who wants to rule and degrade the North, as she has ruled and degraded the South, from the very day of its discovery. There are only very few of the Southern leaders who are not more or less under the influence of the Jesuits, through their wives, family relations, and their friends. Several members of the family of Jeff Davis belong to the Church of Rome.

Even the Protestant ministers are under the influence of the Jesuits without suspecting it. To keep her ascendancy in the North, as she does in the South, Rome is doing here what she has done in Mexico, and in all the South American Republics; she is paralyzing, by a civil war, the arms of the soldiers of Liberty. She divides our nation, in order to weaken, subdue and rule it.

There is a reason the war didn't end as quickly as it should have. Ellen was also writing what the guardians were showing her. Here is her letter:

The North have had no just idea of the strength of the accursed system of slavery. It is this, and this alone, which lies at the foundation of the war. The South have been more and more exacting. They consider it perfectly right to engage in human traffic, to deal in slaves and the souls of men. ...

Thousands have lost their lives, and many have returned to their homes, maimed and crippled for life, their health gone, their earthly prospects forever blighted; and yet how little has been gained! Thousands have been induced to enlist with the understanding that this war was to exterminate slavery; but now that they are fixed, they find that they have been deceived, that the object of this war is not to abolish slavery, but to preserve it as it is. ...

Others have been taken prisoners by the rebels, a fate more to be dreaded than death. ...

The prospects before our nation are discouraging, for there are those filling responsible stations who are rebels at heart. There are commanding officers who are in sympathy with the rebels. While they are desirous of having the Union preserved, they despise those who are antislavery. ...

God is punishing this nation for the high crime of slavery. He has the destiny of the nation in His hands. He will punish the South for the sin of slavery, and the North for so long suffering its overreaching and overbearing influence. ...

The fugitive slave law was calculated to crush out of man every noble, generous feeling of sympathy that should arise in his heart for the oppressed and suffering slave. It was in direct opposition to the teaching of Christ. God's scourge is now upon the North, because they have so long submitted to the advances of the slave power. The sin of Northern proslavery men is great. They have strengthened the South in their sin by sanctioning the extension of slavery; they have acted a prominent part in bringing the nation into its present distressed condition.

The nation was crying out to God, but Ellen was warning all who would listen about the real issues. She goes on:

Some of our leading men in Congress also are constantly working to favor the South. In this state of things, proclamations are issued for national fasts, for prayer that God will bring this war to a speedy and favorable termination. I was then directed to Isaiah 58:5–7: "Is it such a fast that I have chosen? a day for a man to afflict his soul? is it to bow down his head as a bulrush, and to spread sackcloth and ashes under him? wilt thou call this a fast, and an acceptable day to the Lord? Is not this the fast that I have chosen? to loose the bands of wickedness, to undo the heavy burdens, and to let the oppressed go free, and that ye break every yoke? Is it not to deal thy bread to the hungry, and that thou bring the poor that are cast out to thy house? when thou seest the naked, that thou cover him; and that thou hide not thyself from thine own flesh?"

I saw that these national fasts were an insult to Jehovah. He accepts of no such fasts. The recording angel writes in regard to them: "Ye fast for strife and debate, and to smite with the fist of wickedness." I was shown how our leading men have treated the poor slaves who have come to them for protection. Angels have recorded it. Instead of breaking their yoke and letting the oppressed go free, these men have made the yoke more galling for them than when in the service of their tyrannical masters. Love of liberty leads the poor slaves to leave their masters and risk their lives to obtain liberty.
...

God is punishing the North, that they have so long suffered the accursed sin of slavery to exist; for in the sight of heaven it is a sin of the darkest dye. God is not with the South, and He will punish them dreadfully in the end. [Lucifer] is the instigator of all rebellion.

The guardians were asked to get involved in the war at the Battle of Bull Run, which might have led to a quick end to the war, but one of the guardians was asked to interfere and prolong it. Everyone had to see why this judgment had come on this country. At the same time, the guardians were working with President Lincoln to end slavery, while some just wanted to end the war and maintain slavery. It was a battle, but the 13th amendment was passed just before the second inauguration of Lincoln. However, he was clear in his second inaugural address, just as Ellen was clear on the issues of the war.

Here are Lincoln's words from that second inaugural address, inscribed to this day on the walls of the Lincoln Memorial in Washington, D.C.:

Fellow-Countrymen:

At this second appearing to take the oath of the Presidential office there is less occasion for an extended address than there was at the first. Then a statement somewhat in detail of a course to be pursued seemed fitting and proper. Now, at the expiration of four years, during which public declarations have been constantly called forth on every point and phase of the great contest which still absorbs the attention and engrosses the energies of the nation, little that is new could be presented. The progress of our arms, upon which all else chiefly depends, is as well known to the public as to myself, and it is, I trust, reasonably satisfactory and encouraging to all. With high hope for the future, no prediction in regard to it is ventured.

On the occasion corresponding to this four years ago all thoughts were anxiously directed to an impending civil war. All dreaded it, all sought to avert it. While the inaugural address was being delivered from this place, devoted altogether to saving the Union without war, insurgent agents were in the city seeking to destroy it without war—seeking to dissolve the Union and divide effects by negotiation. Both parties deprecated war, but one of them would make war rather than let the nation survive, and the other would accept war rather than let it perish, and the war came.

One-eighth of the whole population were colored slaves, not distributed generally over the Union, but localized in the southern part of it. These slaves constituted a peculiar and powerful interest. All knew that this interest was somehow the cause of the war. To strengthen, perpetuate, and extend this interest was the object for which the insurgents would rend the Union even by war, while the Government claimed no right to do more than to restrict the territorial enlargement of it. Neither party expected for the war the magnitude or the duration which it has already attained. Neither anticipated that the cause of the conflict might cease with or even before the conflict itself should cease. Each looked for an easier triumph, and a result less fundamental and astounding. Both read the same Bible and pray to the same God, and each invokes His aid against the other. It may seem strange that any men should dare to ask a just God's assistance in wringing their bread from the sweat of other men's faces, but let us judge not, that we be not judged. The prayers of both could not be answered. That of neither has been answered fully. The Almighty has His own purposes. "Woe unto the world because of offenses; for it must needs be that offenses come, but woe to that man by whom the offense cometh." If we shall suppose that American slavery is one of those offenses which, in the providence of God, must needs come, but which, having continued through His appointed time, He now wills to remove, and that He gives to both North and South this terrible war as the woe due to those by whom the offense came, shall we discern therein any departure from those divine attributes which the believers in a living God always ascribe to Him? Fondly do we hope, fervently do we pray, that this mighty scourge of war may speedily pass away. Yet, if God wills that it continue until all the wealth piled by the bondsman's two hundred and fifty years of unrequited toil shall be sunk, and until every drop of blood drawn with the lash shall be paid by another drawn with the sword, as was said three thousand years ago, so still it must be said "the judgments of the Lord are true and righteous altogether."

Soon after his second inauguration, Lincoln wrote to his friend Charles, the aforementioned priest: "'Man must not care where and when he will die, provided he dies at the post of honor and duty.' But I may add today, that I have a presentiment that God will call me to Him through the hand of an assassin."

A month after this speech, he was assassinated. This spirit of rebellion and division is swelling again today in this country and inspired by the same rebel leader who starts all wars: Lucifer. He's preparing for one last conflict in which the whole world will be involved.

However, the guardians are preserving this nation a little longer to fulfill its ultimate destiny.

Episode 8

In God We Trust

As the country started to heal after the war, there continued to be attacks to divide it, but the hand of Providence was still working in the midst of this nation. There were consistent attempts to take it down the empire path like many nations before her. One of the most sinister was through the monetary supply. There were attempts at a central bank, an entity that would control the monetary supply of a nation through the 1800s, and success was on and off. Andrew Jackson played heavily in the role of a central bank in the United States.

However, something happened at the dawn of the 20th century. It was King Solomon who said, "The rich rule over the poor, and the borrower is slave to the lender." Additionally, there is a quote most often attributed to the House of Rothschild, the banking lenders of the Old World, which says, "Permit me to issue and control the money of a nation, and I care not who makes its laws!"

It's the cynical golden rule: He who has the gold makes the rules.

Money began to be printed and loaned to this nation, putting it further and further in debt. As World War I began, money was needed to fund it. Industrialization was taking off, and the "Roaring 20s" seemed like the party of prosperity was guaranteed to all, but greed, the love of money, is still the root of all evil.

America has been so central in world events in the past 200 years because she was established to uphold the principles of Jannah; the founding documents describe that. As long as she has maintained these principles, she has been safe. However, a change is coming.

As money was being loaned so easily, the military industrial complex rose up. It was the perfect marriage. War needs money. Money needs war. And how do you distract the world while wars are started and sustained, often under false pretenses? You market things to the public that will supposedly make them happy. After World War II, the Baby Boomer generation lived amid luxuries scarcely dreamed of in history: sex, drugs, rock and roll, and access to information and entertainment like never before. Nevertheless, debt to keep up with the Joneses is still debt, and this indebtedness is still slavery.

President Kennedy saw the dangers. As soon he signed the executive order that would have made the privately owned Federal Reserve unnecessary, thus eliminating interest payments on borrowed funds, it was only a matter of time before the love of money led a man to do one of the most heinous things: taking the life of the leader of the free world. His assassination forever stifled anyone else from challenging that power dynamic.

Everything truly changed for the world in 1944 at Bretton Woods. It was there that world leaders decided to come up with a system to manage foreign exchange that would not put any country at a disadvantage.

It was decided that the world's currencies couldn't be linked to gold, but they could be linked to the U.S. dollar, which was linked to gold. While the U.S. held the gold, other countries held paper currency in U.S. dollars. With more wars to fund, the Federal Reserve printed more and more fiat paper currency. Countries were concerned it would devalue the currency, so they began seeking to convert their dollars into gold. It increased so much that President Nixon decided to delink the U.S. dollar from the gold standard.

Once that happened, printing of fiat currency soared. Fiat currency means "It's as good as we say it is." Today, the majority of the world's money is in U.S dollars. U.S debt has grown over 5,000% since the creation of the Federal Reserve.

When the U.S. got off the gold standard, money began to be loaned to pretty much anyone for anything. The allure of the American Dream was now an allure of the seduction of debt to have the appearance of wealth, just like your neighbors. However, with debt comes burden and stress.

The wealth gap began to grow between the rich and poor like never before. Madison Avenue marketed everything to us, and look at what happened: With increasing debt came a need for both parents to work. Children were no longer being raised by their parents, but by daycare and a failing educational system. That educational system was not teaching young boys and girls how to think, but rather how to be mere reflectors of other people's thoughts. It told them they came from monkeys and life has no purpose.

Values began to decline. The sacredness of marriage slowly eroded. The social contract in America, that unwritten American Dream that, for decades, had worked for so many, was no longer working. Drug use soared; gambling addiction took off; sex saturated the culture; pornography satisfied the lonely; and religion and spirituality lost their luster.

And it's at this moment, when the church loses its power, it turns to power. When the church loses its power, it turns to those in power. When the church loses its power from above, it turns to a power from beneath.

With society unmoored and tensions rising, the religious right saw that they were losing influence. They rejected the voice of the Lamb 2,000 years ago, so it shouldn't be any surprise that they have now, by and large, listened to the whispers of the dragon.

This mingling of church and state, even in free America, was predicted. The prophecies foretold that the professed friends of Jesus would become His enemies.

This nation was to be a safe haven for freedom of conscience. Like a plant, she grew up slowly. She was like a lamb with two horns, but what happens next? She speaks like a dragon, the very symbol of Lucifer.

A nation speaks by her laws, the very principles from which she operates. The beauty of this nation was that it was supposed to protect its minority, though the track record is bad with how we treated the Native Americans, the Japanese, Hispanics, countless minorities, and most of all, African Americans.

How exactly would the nation transform from a lamb to a dragon? Legend says dragons used to eat lambs in the Old World.

How could a nation go from being one who followed the principles of Yeshua to the dictates of Lucifer? A prophecy of Revelation 13 foretells of a time when America would return to the spirit of intolerance and persecution of the empires and superpowers that came before her.

Never forget, this country was to be the guardian of the Protestant spirit; the guardian of conscience in the lives of its citizens, but Revelation 13:17 says a change would come: "No man might buy or sell, save he that had the mark, or the name of the beast, or the number of his name."

There are two things you need to see in these words regarding this power that would arise: 1) It controls the monetary system, but more than that, there is 2) a way to ensure no one can buy or sell without approval of the empire.

Do you see any fulfillment of this happening today? That same spirit that ripped this nation in half 150 years ago—hatred of and prejudice toward others—is striving to gain the victory again today.

Now, let's talk about the mark of the beast. First, the beast is easy: beasts are used to describe empires and kingdoms in history. Thus, we talked about the rise of world empires already, but what is a mark? Cattle are branded; cars are branded; clothing is branded. A company's logo is its mark or trademark.

Does any kingdom, empire, or power on earth today claim to have something that is its mark or brand signature in the realm of the spiritual war? any entity that once was identified as a beast or empire in the prophecies?

Technology may very likely have a role in the enforcement of the mark of the beast, but its ultimately a spiritual allegiance issue: will you and I follow Yeshua or Lucifer? love or selfishness?

The Emperor Constantine knew that uniting a world so divided by religion and practice was nearly impossible. The Christian revolution was a force with which to be reckoned, but he knew this was the only way to maintain global dominance, so he is said to have converted from paganism to Christianity. He then established a weekly day of rest, not on the biblical day of rest, but on the pagan day of worship. It was good for the family, environment, and state of society.

Priest Enright says, "It was the holy Catholic Church that changed the day of rest from Saturday to Sunday, the 1st day of the week. And it not only compelled all to keep Sunday, but at the Council of Laodicea, in AD 364, anathematized – or condemned - those who kept the Sabbath and urged all persons to labor on the 7th day under penalty of anathema."

Since Saturday, the seventh day, not Sunday, is the day specified as a holiday of creation in Scripture, isn't it curious that non-Catholics, who claim to take their religion directly from the Bible, not from the church, observe Sunday instead of Saturday?

C.F. Thomas, Chancellor of Cardinal Gibbons, on October 28, 1895, stated, "Of course the Catholic Church claims that the change [of Sabbath to Sunday] was her act ... And the act is a Mark of her ecclesiastical power and authority in religious matters."

It's her mark of authority. The Christian church today has no basis from Scripture for so many things it teaches or does, and it is this lack of divine authority that has led them to lose their influence in society. However, there are things going on behind the scenes about which you need to know.

Do you notice anything unique about the current political climate? It's increasingly divided. It seems everything has become a political issue: race, wealth, healthcare, environment, and so on. And one could argue, based on the data, the religious right is driving the agenda. They were the deciding voice in the last election.

I want to talk to you about how this prophecy of America eroding freedom of conscience will be fulfilled. Many don't understand how, in free America, morality could be legislated just like it was in the Old World. The prophecies predict that America will abandon the secrets of her power: her lamblike horns. Like Samson cutting off his hair, America will see the sunset of a Protestant Republic, and church and state will unite. This country will repudiate every principle of its Constitution as a Protestant and Republican government.

But how will this happen? Enter ... Christian Reconstructionism?

This is a belief guiding much of the religious right and politics today. This is what is driving them to get so heavily involved in politics, even though Yeshua was adamant that His kingdom was not of this world. They have been deceived into thinking that the only way to usher in the coming of Yeshua is through a conversion of the world, by force if necessary.

A big point of contention is that they have misunderstood spiritual Israel—that anyone and everyone is being called today to walk in the light; to be an heir to the promises and a citizen of Jannah. Instead, they teach and believe the nation of Israel plays a role in prophecy, and this is why there is so much American and evangelical interest in the land of Palestine, specifically Jerusalem. However, Scripture does not teach this.

This is where theories of a secret rapture have come in, when in reality, they have no basis in Scripture. This is why so many who call themselves Christians don't have any interest in caring for the environment. Why would they, if they are on a march to usher in the end of all things and a millennium of peace on the earth?

You can read it for yourself, but here's my point: a deceived base of individuals in America is seeking to regain control and influence for an end-game purpose. I'm here to warn you and make this issue clear before it's too late. They aren't alone. The Society of Jesus is still actively involved in a counter-reformation all these years later, and they nearly have everything in position to take global control once again.

Abortion, immigration, gay marriage—these aren't the real issues where everything is trending. Yes, there is a clear scriptural basis on how to consider these issues, but these aren't the end; they are the means to an end, and that end is legislating morality and destroying freedom of conscience in the United States of America.

There is an expression: "Never let a good crisis go to waste." Author Chris Hedges describes it like this:

> ... the empowerment of the Christian fascists. They are what comes next. For decades they have been organizing to take power. They have built infrastructures and organizations, including lobbying groups, schools and universities as well as media platforms, to prepare.

They have seeded their cadre into the political system. The left, meanwhile, has seen its institutions and organizations destroyed or corrupted by corporate power.

The Christian fascists, as in all totalitarian movements, need a crisis, manufactured or real, in order to seize power. This crisis may be financial. It could be triggered by a catastrophic terrorist attack. Or it could be the result of a societal breakdown from our climate emergency. The Christian fascists are poised to take advantage of the chaos, or perceived chaos.

They are waiting for a crisis. America must be taken to a breaking point, most likely by economic turmoil, and once she breaks, then a time of trouble will begin, but what does that look like?

Today, multitudes are being led to believe that desire is the highest law, license is liberty, and a person is accountable only to oneself. However, in reality, anarchy is seeking to sweep away all law—not only divine, but also human. The centralizing of wealth and power; the vast combinations for the enriching of the few at the expense of the many; the combinations of the poorer classes for the defense of their interests and claims; the spirit of unrest, riot, and bloodshed; the worldwide dissemination of the same teachings that led to the French Revolution—all are tending to involve the whole world in a struggle similar to that which convulsed France.

Then you and I will see the prophecy fulfilled. To control and reverse the ability of someone to buy or sell, you need to first control the monetary system and then have a surveillance and technological apparatus in place that would limit someone's ability to access his or her bank account, all linked to one's biometric data: fingerprints, facial recognition, whatever.

Noam Chomsky recently commented on Shoshana Zuboff's book, The Age of Surveillance Capitalism, which, in his view, best predicts and outlines the techno-surveillance system that has already begun to take hold in the U.S. and beyond, as companies such as Google, Amazon, and others find novel ways to exert control over humankind.

In the book, Zuboff lays bare the threats to 21st-century society: a controlled "hive" of total connection that seduces with promises of total certainty for maximum profit at the expense of democracy, freedom, and our human future.

Chomsky commented on this idea:

> The kind of model toward which society is moving is already illustrated to a substantial extent in China, where they have very heavy surveillance systems and … what they call a social credit system,". "You get a certain number of points, and if you, say, jaywalk, violate a traffic rule, you lose points. If you help an old lady across the street, you gain points. Pretty soon, all this gets internalized, and your life is dedicated to making sure you follow the rules that are established. This is going to expand enormously as we move to what's called the internet of things, meaning every device around you— your refrigerator, your toothbrush and so on—is picking up information about what you're doing, predicting what you're going to do next, trying to control what you're going to do next, advise what you do next.

As I see it, Lucifer is seeking to be god. His path forward is to obtain the three great powers of God: omniscience—knowing everything through mass data collection; omnipresence—the ability to see what's happening everywhere at once via wholesale surveillance; and omnipotence—the ultimate power to control someone's ability through the two previous apparatuses; to turn someone off if that person doesn't align with the new laws of society.

And yet, we are told the guardians have been tasked with holding back this dystopian world control and calamity until everyone clearly understands the issues at stake. However, when they get the signal to let go, there will be such a scene of strife that no pen can depict it. Are you ready for that?

I hope you are seeing the issues in the controversy so clearly that you can make a decision regarding whose side you want to join before it's too late.

With that said, next, I need to tell you about the coming invasion.

Episode 9

The Black Swan

The present is a time of overwhelming interest to everyone living. Rulers and statemen, those who occupy positions of trust and authority, thinking men and women of all classes, have their attention fixed upon the events taking place around us. They are watching the strained, restless relations that exist among the nations. They observe the intensity that is taking possession of every earthly element and recognize that something great and decisive is about to take place—that the world is on the verge of a stupendous crisis.

Where do you see the world trending? If we stepped back and saw the bigger picture, what would we see? Why has the cosmic war continued for so long? Will it ever come to an end?

Many people can turn on the news today and come away with less and less hope. We see a world no longer in touch with the land and nature, yet obsessed to save it.

When this nation was founded, pretty much everyone was a farmer. Now, few people even know a farmer. Additionally, did you know farmers have some of the highest suicide rates of any occupation? What in the world is going on?

One of my favorite books says something worthwhile about the original plan for mankind:

> Every family had a home on the land, with sufficient ground for growing food. Thus were provided both the means and the incentive for a useful, industrious, and self-supporting life. And no devising of men has ever improved upon that plan. To the world's departure from it is owing, to a large degree, the poverty and wretchedness that exist today.

Today, though we are closer in distance to each other than ever before, we are further apart as a society. Social media is the drug that lonely souls are craving, and all eyes are on America. We have access to all that we need to realize all the pieces are coming together. The Constitution that has served America so well seems under increasing scrutiny.

Pope Pius IX, in his Encyclical Letter of August 15, 1854, said, "The absurd and erroneous doctrines or ravings in defense of liberty of conscience are a most pestilential error—a pest, of all others, most to be dreaded in a state." The same pope, in his Encyclical Letter of December 8, 1864, applied the term "heretic" to "those who assert the liberty of conscience and of religious worship," and also "all such as maintain that the church may not employ force."

Earlier, we talked about systems of control being put in place, but how could that be implemented on a global scale? Could it perhaps be by the same power that has 1,000 military bases on the earth in over 80 countries? America today is the sole superpower.

Furthermore, by the decree of enforcing the institution of the papacy in violation of the law of God, America will disconnect herself fully from righteousness. Can you imagine a day when morality could be legislated in this nation?

When America repudiates every principle of its Constitution as a Protestant and Republican government, then you and I may know that the time has come for the marvelous working of Lucifer, and the end is near.

There have been attempts to bring all of this into our ranks many times in recent years, but the winds of disruption are being held back by the guardians. However, when there are enough representatives to stand for the truth and light, then the winds will be let go.

When that happens, we must be ready to stand through a time of trouble. It is not a far-distant fantasy. Yeshua described the signs for when things would be loosening, so for what should we be looking? A black swan.

A black swan is an extremely rare event with severe consequences. It cannot be predicted beforehand, though many claim it should be predictable after the fact. It's that unlooked for, unexpected crisis we talked about earlier.

Political unrest, calamities, earthquakes, storms, famines, pestilence, pandemics, nature crying out—all of these are ingredients, but there must be a crisis-triggering event—a black swan event—something so out of the ordinary that no one can predict its timing or magnitude. Much of the Christian world is denying the signs of the times, such as societal and environmental collapse, because they disagree with the causes. Whether you call it climate change, a climate catastrophe, or, as Al Gore says, "Every night when you turn on the news, it's like taking a nature hike through the book of Revelation," many recognize something is happening.

Lucifer has studied the secrets of the laboratories of nature, and he uses all his power to control the elements as far as Jah allows. When he was permitted to afflict a man named Job, how quickly flocks and herds, servants, houses, children, were swept away, one trouble succeeding another as in a moment!

The Scriptures are not silent on this moment: "At that time, Michael shall stand up, the great prince which stands watch over the children of thy people - and there shall be a time of trouble such as never was since there was a nation - even up to that time. And at that time, the faithful will be delivered - everyone whose name is written in the book of life" (Daniel 12:1).

However, this is all leading up to something. For the last 50 or more years, the world has been prepared, step by step, piece by piece, moment by moment, for what is just ahead of us. How were we prepared? The best way to persuade people is actually based on a biblical teaching: by beholding, we become changed.

Therefore, if Yeshua, aka Jesus, was most passionately exclamatory to His followers that at the close of time, more than anything else don't be deceived, then how would the deception of nearly 8 billion people take place? One step at a time.

I want you to think about what has formed your worldview. What has made you who you are and how you think?

The biggest influences in our lives are upbringing, education, religion, and media. Most of us, for the last 50 years, were raised by media because our parents were busy keeping up with the Joneses, so there goes that potential of parenting and values. With that said, where do we look next? Education.

For nearly 50 years, children have not been taught **how** to think, but **what** to think; to prepare for a manufacturing-type, receptive work career. We were told we wouldn't walk around in life with a calculator, yet that's exactly what we all have in our pockets: a calculator, computer, personal assistant, TV, and whatever else our phones do for us.

For the most part, we were taught we came from monkeys, primordial ooze, or a big bang, so we have no real, eternal purpose. We are random chemicals, so we fight disease with random chemicals rather than believe we were created from the dust of the ground and the healthiest way to live is getting food from the dust of the ground. We eat food from a manufacturing plant, rather than from a plant that grows in our backyards. Okay, I'll step off that soap box.

Well, not yet. We grew up on cartoons and imagery of farms and food; now, it's all aliens and robots that dominate our media. What once was the Partridge family is now the Adams family or, let's be honest, really no family. We were told that living life to the fullest is in the big city, not with the uneducated farmers.

Religion? Well, we've covered that: it's failed us for the most part.

Lastly, I don't want to miss the role of media, specifically, American media, which has positioned the nation as the leader in all young minds around the world for 50 years. Think of every disaster movie, alien contact movie, etc. America is the nation to which to look for hope and answers.

And where is all of this propaganda leading us? We've been brainwashed in order to prepare us for what is coming, such as making contact with super-intelligent, advanced beings from another realm and finding out that death is not the end.

Lucifer is herding people into the cities to control them. Whether supernaturally or through the use of means to manipulate the weather, he's able to cause earthquakes, tsunamis, hurricanes, tornadoes, and wildfires. He has these powers, and they will continue to intensify.

However, let's talk about what he's setting up. So many people lately are becoming "spiritual." They have no defense to superstition or mysticism, so they are open to anything the paranormal can make appear as real, and that is where it's going to get real.

All these disasters are going to be used to manipulate and intimidate. All the tactics of biowarfare and eroding the nutritional value in the food supply make for a sick society. Lucifer professed to be seeking to promote the stability of the divine government in Jannah, while secretly bending every effort to secure its overthrow. He is using the same tactics of ages past. We can hear the news cycle even starting to ramp up what was once a conspiracy: that we are on the verge of making contact with intelligent alien life; but what if it's just

Lucifer sending his legions to earth to represent beings from far-distant galaxies?

If the news and NASA are to be believed, then intelligent alien life will appear to make contact very soon. How would you react if you turned on the news, and it was announced that we have made contact with ancestors and loved ones from another dimension? Could the gods of legend and the world's religions appear in the great urban centers of the world?

Without any defense, all the religions will be deceived. These intelligent beings will declare that Jah has sent them to convince the rejecters of the global agenda of a new way of doing things, a new order of the ages, with a call to save this planet we call home by whatever means necessary. What will be the proposed answer to our troubles? Could it be like the time before, when religion and government were combined and proposed a global day of rest for mankind and the environment? This was Constantine's rationale to enact a new day of rest, Sunday, because nature needed a day of rest from humanity.

How would you react if these spirits, ancestors, and impersonated relatives passionately expressed sorrow for the destruction of the planet and agreed with the testimony of religious teachers that the degraded state of morals is caused by the desecration of Sunday and a disregard for the environment? Through fear or force, Lucifer always endeavors to rule the conscience and to secure homage to himself.

We await one last deception. Could it be possible that those who honor the seventh day, the holiday of creation, will be denounced as enemies of law and order who break down the moral restraints of society, cause anarchy and corruption, and call down the judgments of God upon the earth, even being accused as the cause of climate catastrophe? Could they be pronounced as traitors, terrorists, fundamentalists, and enemies of the state?

For thousands of years, men, women, boys, and girls have cried out to Jah and Yeshua to intervene in world affairs, but before judgment is pronounced once and for all and the fate of everyone is decided, there must be a call that goes out to everyone currently enslaved and deceived by the system of Babylon the Great.

For too long, we have been entranced by her music and stories, as well as commercials that tell us we won't be happy unless we go into more debt to buy one more thing.

I know this all sounds strange as we sit on the edge of the greatest technological revolution in history. It seems we are on the verge of the best times ever ... to some, but not all.

Technology can do amazing things ... until it's in the hands of the wrong person or persons. Today, we know technology is tracking everything. It's the omnipotence Lucifer always wanted; the omnipresence he never had; the omniscience he craves; to be everywhere; to know everything; to have all power over someone's life. You think it's your savior, but is it? I know I've thought it was, but is it?

Picture this: Calamities start to destroy entire cities; there aren't enough funds to bail them out; insurance companies go bust; there is widespread crop failure, which results in malnutrition and a global pandemic. The economy today is so fragile that even one significant global calamity could bring it to its knees. We have seen that recently. You already have the current wealth gap between the rich and the poor, and that tension is at a fever pitch. What do you think will happen if people don't have their food delivered on trucks and set nicely on grocery store shelves like always? I think we can only expect rioting in the streets in a moment of chaos like that.

And we know that doesn't last long. There are people in position to seize on that chaos. We talked about that already. When they do, there will be a revolution much like what I have described to you. Everything is in place.

It is in that moment, that fragile moment, when the overmastering delusion will take place. Even now, they are already releasing bits and pieces of what awaits us through our film, television, and news cycles.

How do you think Lucifer and his legion are going to come and deceive the whole world? Their main M.O. to lie, propagating they don't even exist. Thus, how do you deceive such intelligent humans? Could it be through the gods they worship—the god of science and the goddess of technology? The priests of science and innovation are already prophesying of what's coming.

Project BlueBook, recently declassified, shows us over 12,000 accounts of UFOs released by the U.S. Government. Could it be that Lucifer is going to make it appear that a Messiah has returned? What of the prophecy that "every eye shall see him"?

Diana Pasulka, author of **UFOs, Religion and Technology**, says the following:

> We're in a kind of planetary crisis at the moment, and there's an increase in apocalyptic beliefs about our capacity to survive on earth. A lot of people see disaster on the horizon, and there's a deep fear that we won't be able to save ourselves.
>
> So what will save us? Well, for some, it will be these advanced beings who come to us and tell us what we can do or how we can escape. Maybe they will help us find another planetary home, or maybe they'll bring some lifesaving technology. Who knows? But these sorts of beliefs are lurking beneath a lot of the popular fascination with alien life.
>
> And think about what many religions consist of: Often, a religion begins with contact from something divine, something beyond the normal plane of human experience, and that thing communicates with a person on earth. And then there's a story told about it. And then from that story, we get a larger narrative that erupts into what we call religious traditions.
>
> Something very similar is happening right now around belief in extraterrestrial life. What fascinates me about this new form of religion is that scientists and people

who generally distance themselves from things like miracles seem to embrace this new religious form.

If we were to learn that alien life exists, it would completely upend the religious worldview right?

She goes on to say"

I spend a lot of time at the Vatican, and there are people there like astronomer Guy Consolmagno – A Jesuit and Director of the Vatican Observatory and author of the book Would You Baptize an Extraterrestrial? who wouldn't blink an eye if alien life suddenly appeared.

She concludes with:

Who knew that the Vatican owned an observatory run by Jesuit scientists? Or how about what Guy Consolmagno actually says where he shared (and I quote) "that we are soon to be visited by an alien savior from another world.

The Bible has a few warnings about the end of the war:

Let no man deceive you by any means: for that day shall not come, except there come a falling away first, and that man of sin be revealed, the son of perdition; Who opposes and exalts himself above all that is called God, or that is worshipped; so that he as God sits in the temple of God, showing himself that he is God. ... And then shall that wicked be revealed, whom the Lord shall consume with the spirit of his mouth, and shall destroy with the brightness of his coming: Even him, whose coming is after the working of Satan with all power and signs and lying wonders, And with all deceivableness of unrighteousness in them that perish; because they received not the love of the truth, that they might be saved. And for this cause God shall send them strong delusion, that they should believe a lie. (2 Thessalonians ١١-٨, ٤, ٣: ٢)

For such are false apostles, deceitful workers, transforming themselves into the apostles of Christ. And no marvel; for Satan himself is transformed into an angel of light. Therefore it is no great thing if his ministers also be transformed as the ministers of righteousness; whose end shall be according to their works. (2 Corinthians 11:13–15)

If you look at what Jesus (Yeshua) says about the end of the world, He keeps one note very clear: don't be deceived. Why all the warnings?

Now the Spirit speaks expressly, that in the latter times some shall depart from the faith, giving heed to seducing spirits, and doctrines of devils [other versions say "by demons"—legions of fallen angels]. (1 Timothy 4:1)

But though we, or an angel from heaven, preach any other gospel unto you than that which we have preached unto you, let him be accursed. As we said before, so say I now again, if any man preaches any other gospel unto you than that ye have received, let him be accursed. (Galatians 1:8, 9)

What would happen if the very men who wrote the Scriptures were impersonated by these lying spirits? What would happen if they appeared to contradict what they wrote? What if they denied the divine origin of the Scriptures, thus tearing away the foundation of truth and putting out the light that reveals the way back to Jannah?

Lucifer is making the world believe that the Scriptures are mere fiction, or at least a book suited to the infancy of the race, but now to be lightly regarded or cast aside as obsolete. And to take the place of the Scriptures, he holds out spiritual manifestations. Here is a channel wholly under his control.

This age-old religion of spiritualism, in which you can do whatever you want and still find your way back to the city of Jannah, is prevalent more than ever. While it formerly denounced the Scriptures, spiritualism now professes to accept both, but the Scriptures are interpreted in a manner that are pleasing to the unrenewed heart, while its solemn and vital truths are made of no effect.

Love is dwelt upon as the chief attribute of God, but it is degraded to a weak sentimentalism, making little distinction between good and evil, right and wrong. Justice, denunciation of sin and selfishness, and the requirements of the law of Jannah are all kept out of sight. Does that religion of spiritualism sound familiar? To me, it sounds like much of modern-day Christianity.

While Lucifer seems to be doing all he can to destroy the cities of the world, what would happen if he was preaching and promoting a message of peace? While it may appear that he is professing to seek to promote the stability of the divine government, secretly, he is always bending every effort to secure its overthrow.

Furthermore, the churches are going to think they are doing Jannah a service by trying to force the consciences of millions, whether for the environment or moral reasons. Could the dignitaries of church and state unite to bribe, persuade, or compel all classes to honor Sunday as a day for the god of nature? The lack of divine authority will be supplied by oppressive enactments.

Political corruption is destroying the love of justice and regard for truth, and even in free America, rulers and legislators, in order to secure public favor, will yield to the popular demand for a law enforcing Sunday observance. Liberty of conscience, which has cost so great a sacrifice, will no longer be respected.

I hear Christians talking about a millennium of peace, but it's all a deception.

I want to touch again on the deception. With all the talk of UFOs and contact with intelligent alien life, it seems it's no longer a matter of "if," but "when."

I went down the rabbit hole about a year ago regarding what happens to people who say they have experienced an "alien abduction." This is what I found:

Did you know the only stated cure for the repeated PTSD of someone who has been abducted by aliens is to call out in the name of Jesus for help? Did you know there are only two common themes in all messages from the legions ... I mean aliens? They are 1) Yeshua (Jesus) is not who He says He is, and 2) the Scriptures can't be trusted. I find that strangely similar to the underlying agenda of Lucifer throughout this story through which we have been going.

However, no one can now imagine how vulnerable people will soon be. For Lucifer to succeed in the work of deception, it must be so subtle and powerful that it will overwhelm the human race, both with its rationality and attraction. Consider the event of an offer by visitors from an advanced civilization on another planet for assistance to a perishing human race confronted with war, crime, violence, pollution, pandemic, climate change, genocide, and a host of other ills that mankind's rebellion and selfishness have produced? It will seem irresistible.

Science has all but promised contact will happen—not if, but when. With all the propaganda of the media and the use of fear-based messaging, the world is already susceptible to this delusion of beings contacting us with a message, perhaps telling us they created us and want to save us—our own savior who doesn't commission us to cease from being selfish. They can promise a new age, where all is peace and love; that all religion is one. Unlike most religions, the UFO-and-alien phenomenon is already being baptized by the religion of science.

This is what some of the leading researchers in this field are already saying:

> One theory which can no longer be taken very seriously is that UFOs are Interstellar spaceships.

> [Alien Abductions] often accompanied by sadistic sexual manipulation, is reminiscent of the medieval tales of encounters with demons.

> The UFO manifestations seem to be, by and large, merely minor variations of the age-old demonological phenomenon.

I see nothing in the alien abduction phenomenon which cannot be explained in the Biblically known abilities and deceptive agenda of fallen angels.

What might an advanced extraterrestrial civilization want from us? One of the primary motivations for the exploration of the New World was to convert the inhabitants to Christianity – peacefully if possible – forceful if necessary. Can we exclude the possibility of an extraterrestrial evangelism? (Dr. Carl Sagan)

Abductees are often told that "a cataclysmic change is coming ... – it will be the time when the disasters are at their peak. ... The remainder of the people who are living will be picked up by spacecraft and be taken to safety."

In the last scenes of this earth's history, war seems more and more likely. There will be more and more pestilence, pandemic, plague, and famine. The waters of the deep will overflow their boundaries. Property and life will be destroyed by fire and flood.

Should we be preparing for the mansions that Yeshua has gone to prepare for us in Jannah?

Before this is all over, Lucifer is going to appear as a benefactor of the race, healing the diseases of the people and professing to present a new and more exalted system of religious faith; but at the same time, he will work as a destroyer.

As the crowning act in the great drama of deception, Lucifer himself will personate Yeshua—the Christ; Maitreya; Krisnha; Jesus; Issa; Messiah—for whom all major religions have been professing to look at the time of the second advent as the consummation of their hopes. At that time, the great deceiver will make it appear that the Christ has come.

In different parts of the earth, Lucifer will manifest himself among people as a majestic being of dazzling brightness, resembling the description of Yeshua given by John in the Revelation. The glory that surrounds him will be unsurpassed by anything that human eyes have ever seen.

Imagine scrolling and seeing a Facebook livestream or turning on the news and hearing the shouts of triumph ring out upon the air: "Christ has come! The Messiah is here!" What would you do? How would you respond to seeing people prostrate themselves in adoration before him, while he lifts up his hands and pronounces a blessing upon them, as Christ blessed His disciples when He was upon the earth?

Imagine hearing his voice as soft and subdued, yet full of melody, in gentle, compassionate tones, presenting some of the same gracious, heavenly truths that Yeshua uttered; imagine seeing him heal the diseases of the people; imagine a global pandemic and a Messiah figure who can heal anyone who is sick; and then, in his assumed character of Christ, he claims to have changed the weekly holiday to celebrate the creation, from Sabbath to Sunday, and commands all to honor the day that he has blessed.

How would you react if you heard him state that those who persist in keeping holy the seventh day are blaspheming his name by refusing to listen to his legions sent to them with light and truth? This will be the strong, almost overmastering delusion before the last chapter of our story is written.

Episode 10

Earth 2.0

How does this story end?

Imagine a planet in chaos. Ancestors, friends, family—all our loved ones seeming to come back from the dead, starting to appear all over the world, and making contact with us. How about diseases being healed instantly, yet war is raging and nature is seemingly out of control?

The argument will be raised that this all could end if that one little group of traitors, those rebels claiming conscience over culture, would fall in line. Their supposed infidelity is spiraling the world into extinction.

Pen cannot depict and word cannot describe what lies before us. As the calamities continue, nature rips apart at the seams, and the economy struggles to maintain our temporal prosperity, could America's lawmakers eventually feel as though they have no other choice than to appease the protestors on both sides—the one that sees anything as progress in the name of preventing environmental catastrophe and the one that claims an angry is God offended by the moral decay of society?

The truth is that the being most Christians describe as God today is no better than Baal, the sun god of Phoenicia. If the way you describe something or someone is not actually who that person or thing is, then it's a fantasy; it's not real.

For a time, it will seem that new laws to appease the masses at the expense of the few are the solution. Lucifer will make it appear like that, anyway. Imagine if new laws were enacted in America, and the nation's calamities and pestilences ceased. Then the rest of the world will follow and remove liberty of conscience in a moment if that is truly all that is needed to stop this crisis.

Then imagine that while this is happening, the future citizens of Jannah—by the grace of Jah, that includes you and me—will be sharing a contrarian message that all will hear loud and clear.

When someone gets on the microphone to declare peace, security, and safety, that's usually a time to be concerned. It's only the intervention of the guardians that keeps global chaos from breaking out today.

In this last crisis, we are told many people will lose their lives; many will be imprisoned for their desire to stand for principle. This is not new. Men, women, boys, and girls throughout history who stood for something often laid down their lives so that the tree of liberty was refreshed from time to time with the blood of the saints. However, those who stand for principle and conscience will see their reward—perhaps not immediately, but one day.

We are promised at that time that any who are imprisoned will be visited by the guardians. At that time, many will hear the message loud and clear, more by what they witness than by words.

Babylon and all of her systems of selfishness, corruption, greed, and evil will be laid open for all to see, and in a moment, she will be no more. Revelation tells us that there will be seven judgments poured out onto the world—on all those who chose selfishness over love. All those who thought they could save themselves will be sorely disappointed.

In the streets of Jannah, there will be no song of this nature sung: "To me that loved myself, and washed myself, redeemed myself, unto me be glory and honor, blessing and praise." However, this is the keynote of the song that is sung by many here in this world. They do not know what it means to be meek and lowly in heart; and they do not intend to know this if they can avoid it.

In light of the fact that so many claim the name of Christianity and yet deny it in their actions, there will be some surprises in Jannah. There will be many who have not heard the names of Yeshua or Jah.

However, these rescued ones have cherished the principles they learned in nature and from what was revealed to them, and to many, those revelations will be in dreams. Some will ask Yeshua, when they meet him for the first time, "What are these wounds in your hands?" The response from Him will be, "I got these in the house of my friends." Once we are rescued from a planet in chaos we will live in the city of Jannah for 1,000 years.

During that time, all will have a chance to ask the hard questions: Where is my friend? my son? my sister? my father? my husband? my wife? my boyfriend? my girlfriend? We will make sense of all that currently doesn't. Then we will one day return to earth.

The city of Jannah will relocate to earth 2.0. When we return, we are told we will see the world in ruins; the cities that Lucifer destroyed; everything. Yeshua will raise the dead of all ages, but Lucifer will make it appear that he has raised them with his power. He will marshal the armies of all the earth for one last battle. He does not even state who he is in that moment, yet still hides behind a disguise. He will claim to be the prince, the rightful ruler of the world; that he is their redeemer and is now going to rescue them from the invaders in the golden city of Jannah. He points them to the millions around and how they clearly outnumber those in the city.

Lucifer will work miracles. The giants of old, the brilliance of ages gone by—all will be on display. Kings, generals who conquered nations, ambitious warriors whose approach made kingdoms tremble—all will be ready for battle. They pick up the train of thought that they had before falling in battle—that same desire of survival of the fittest conquest. They will all plan one last attack.

Those in the city will be watching. This will take some time. Strangely enough, we are told that the gates of the city will be open, yet none will enter. The billions outside the city will instead make weapons of war. Generals will marshal all into companies and divisions, but then something will arrest their attention. Up in the sky, like a panorama film, all will watch this story that I have just shared with you; all will see the part they acted; all will see when they made the decision to turn from love and accept selfishness and desire as their ruling principle.

Yeshua will stand up and reveal those closest to the throne as those who were once most zealous in the cause of Lucifer. The coronation of the King of all kings takes place. All will bow and acknowledge this is just and true. Even Lucifer will recall the moment he chose selfishness over love.

Everyone from all ages will be watching this moment. Yeshua will then declare, "Behold the purchase of My blood! For these, I suffered; for these, I died, that they might dwell in My presence throughout eternal ages." In this moment, millions will turn and look at their spiritual leaders—many pastors, priests, imams, and teachers who have misled them.

Lucifer believes that perhaps even now, he can stir up a revolt. As he attempts it, he is finally unmasked. All the earth turns on him, and in this moment, it will all end at the mercy of Yeshua. After this moment, every tear will be wiped away.

Those in the city will watch the earth be recreated, much more beautifully than ever before.

We are told we will have a place in the city and a place on our own land outside the city, with animals to love, not eat; food to enjoy; friends with which to enjoy it. If you like to travel, imagine the destinations to explore; the food; the adventure. Every faculty will be developed; every capacity increased. The acquirement of knowledge will not weary the mind or exhaust the energies.

There, the grandest enterprises may be carried forward; the loftiest aspirations reached; the highest ambitions realized; and still, there will arise new heights to surmount, new wonders to admire, new truths to comprehend, and fresh objects to call forth the powers of mind, soul, and body.

If you can find joy here, you will find it tenfold there. All of which you've ever dreamed and yet with which you've been unsatisfied will be a reality there.

Well, that's the end of the story. Thank you for taking the time to watch and listen. I imagine you have many questions; at least I hope you do. There were so many people who helped make this a reality. Why? Pretty much for one reason.

My request to you, or maybe even a challenge to you, is to ask yourself, 'Is this true? If so, what does that mean for me?'

If this story is true, on which side of the war do you find yourself? on which side do you **want** to be found?

If what you have heard is even intriguing, I invite you to continue the journey. However, if what you've heard isn't for you, then at least you can better understand some of the ideas and concepts that are shaping world events and geopolitics in our world today and perhaps tomorrow.

If you have any questions, I'd love to hear from you. How? (need contact info)

-   Jared

For contact information, to watch this series for free, or to order copies of this book – Go to Loveandwarstory.com

Made in the USA
Columbia, SC
12 August 2020